Chesapeake Crimes I

Chesapeake Crimes I

Coordinating editor:
Donna Andrews

Editorial Panel:
Martha Pennigar, Cindy Silberblatt, and
Elizabeth Sheley

Additional editorial support
by Marcia Talley
and other members of the Board of Directors,
Chesapeake Chapter, Sisters in Crime

2d revised edition

Library of Congress Cataloging-in-Publication Data

Chesapeake Crimes I; 2d rev. ed. / coordinating editor,
Donna Andrews.

    p. cm.

ISBN-978-1-4303-0525-5

1.   Detective and mystery stories, American. 2.
    American fiction – Women authors. I. Andrews,
    Donna.

PS648.D4C54 2006

Front cover photograph ©2006 by David Stybr

Back cover photograph ©2006 by Ron Belanger

Cover design ©2006 by Barbara Parker

Table of Contents

FOREWORD

by Laura Lippman

The notion of chapter pride should be antithetical to an organization such as Sisters in Crime. The name is plain. We are sisters—with quite a few brothers, actually—who have come together to support writers at every stage of their careers. From the shy neophyte trying to find the confidence to start, to writers who have been recognized as the standard-bearers of the mystery genre, we are family, just like the song says. (And you have no idea how painful it is for a Baltimore Orioles fan to allude to the Sister Sledge tune that became Pittsburgh's anthem in the 1979 World Series.)

Still, I hope you'll forgive me if I crow a bit over my own chapter, the Chesapeake Sisters in Crime, fifteen of whom are showcased here in

Chesapeake Crimes. Chesapeake SinC members have won every major mystery award given in the last decade, including the Edgar, Agatha, Anthony, Macavity, Shamus and the Nero Wolfe. You will find some of those award winners here. I'll offer even odds that there are just as many future award winners among the contributors, possibly for the stories in this very volume.

You will also find a range of stories that accommodate every mystery taste, from cozy to hardboiled, from humorous to dark. Donna Andrews' reluctant sleuth, Meg Langslow, is drawn into yet another homicide investigation against her will in "Night Shades"—while working with some guest stars in the niftiest bit of cross-casting since the detectives from "Homicide" and "Law and Order" teamed up. Elizabeth Foxwell, known for her historical short stories, delivers a haunting tale in "Grave Ends," while Maria Lima serves up "The Butler Didn't Do It," injecting fresh blood into the oh-so-traditional English manor house mystery. Marcia Talley offers "Vital Signs," a bittersweet story that reminds us that a crime's legacy does not necessarily end when a crime is solved. And, finally, Elaine Viets' "Wedding Knife" provides a motive for murder that will be plausible to every woman between the ages of 18 and 80. I could write a heartfelt recommendation for every story in this collection, but why should I take up more space when you have so much good reading ahead of you?

If one commonality emerges in Chesapeake Crimes, it is family, not geography. That's fitting, I think. This is much too proper an anthology to quote directly the famous Philip Larkin poem about parents, so let's just say that mom and dad can, um, mess you up—along with aunts and uncles, nieces and nephews, husbands and wives. We are family. And while I don't have all my sisters with me in this anthology, I do have a choice group that showcases the depth, breadth and versatility of the Chesapeake Sisters in Crime.

Laura Lippman
Baltimore, Maryland
November 2003

NIGHT SHADES

by Donna Andrews

"Meg, do you have an aunt Matilda?" my friend Hollis asked.

"Well, yes and no," I said, shifting the phone to my other shoulder as I rinsed a glass. "I used to—a great-aunt, actually—but she died about a month ago."

"Yes, I know," Hollis said. "Only she didn't die. She was murdered."

I sighed, and rubbed my forehead. I could feel a headache starting. These days all my relatives, having declared me a brilliant amateur sleuth, brought me mysteries to solve every time I turned around. I, of course, reacted with the same enthusiasm I showed when the cat dragged in a dead vole.

But that was my family. I'd always thought Hollis Ball one of the most sensible, down-to-earth people I'd never met.

"How do you know she was murdered?" I asked.

A pause. A lengthy pause. I could hear country western music playing somewhere in the background.

"You're probably going to think I'm crazy," she said.

"You haven't met my family, have you?"

"She told me."

"Aunt Matilda?"

"That's right," Hollis said.

"She told you?" I said. "Look, the way I heard it, she keeled over in the middle of the night from a chronic heart condition; it's not as if she had time for dramatic deathbed revelations. When did she tell you?"

"You're not going to believe this."

"Try me."

"About an hour ago."

It was my turn for the lengthy pause.

"You're calling from a bar somewhere, aren't you?" I asked, finally.

"Look, I know it sounds incredible, but hear me out."

"Holl, why don't you go home and get some sleep and we'll talk about this in the morning. If you still think it was murder."

"Murder? What murder?" came a voice from behind me.

Damn. I'd thought my Dad was already asleep. If I'd known he was going to pop into the kitchen for a bedtime snack, I'd have been more careful about uttering the M-word aloud. Decades of mystery reading had given him an insatiable craving to get involved in real, live homicide investigations.

"Here," I said, handing him the phone. "It's Hollis Ball. She thinks Aunt Matilda was murdered. You talk to her."

Dad and Hollis exchanged loud greetings. Good, I thought; I'll let Dad talk some sense into her. I went back to scrubbing the kitchen. Dad was staying with me for a few days while doing some research on poisonous plants at the Library of Congress. He'd insisted on paying for my hospitality by cooking dinner every night. Tonight's spaghetti bolognese had transformed the kitchen into something resembling a crime scene. And he'd promised lasagna tomorrow. Perhaps I should simply repaint the walls tomato red. Or talk someone into inviting us over for dinner tomorrow. Better yet, meet some friends in a restaurant, where even Dad wouldn't insist on helping out in the kitchen. Yes, that was the ticket. I was scouring my social circle for candidates when I heard Dad utter the ominous words:

"Of course! I understand completely. Yes, I'm sure Meg knows where Toby's bar is. We'll come right away."

φ

"You want another of those?"

I glanced up to see Hollis's cousin Toby looming over me. When I was sober, Toby's size, demeanor, and excessive hairiness made me just a little nervous. But after the two excellent margaritas he'd mixed for me, I was beginning to warm to him. He was as daft as the rest of them, of course, but at least he kept bringing me drinks and popcorn and only expressed his disappointment in me with a stony stare.

"Sure," I said, handing him my empty glass. "Why not?"

Dad, on my left, and Hollis, on my right, were pointedly ignoring me. And talking with great animation to the two empty chairs across the table. The two chairs occupied, according to them, by the ghosts of Hollis's deceased ex-husband, Sam, and my dear departed Aunt Matilda. Thank goodness the only other denizens of the bar were two locals already so intoxicated that conversing with furniture probably seemed normal to them.

Dad and Hollis were ready for another round, too—his bald head was beginning to shine with sweat, and she was gesturing grandly with her empty glass. Toby collected their empties, along with the untouched margaritas he'd placed in front of the two vacant chairs. Sam, I noted, had ostensibly gone through two margaritas, while Aunt Matilda, true to form, was on her fourth. Or maybe it was the other way around. Not that either glass showed the slightest signs of being sipped.

"Hang on," I said, catching Toby's arm as he passed by and snagging one of the untouched margaritas. "Why don't I just finish off one of these?"

"Be my guest," he said. "You won't like it."

"Why not?" I asked, as I lifted the glass.

"Ghosts suck all the goodness out of food and drink, if you let them," Hollis explained. "It'll taste...well, it won't be the same."

To my surprise, she was right. It wasn't same crisp, perfect margarita I'd been drinking. It was...flat? Stale? Off somehow. Although I knew ghosts had nothing to do with it. Obviously Toby made the ghosts' drinks with cheap, house tequila, and saving the good stuff for the humans. I was relieved to know he wasn't pouring his best tequila down the drain just to humor Dad and Hollis.

"You're right: it isn't the same," I said, raising an eyebrow at Toby. "I guess I'll have a fresh one, if you don't mind."

Toby took the rejected glass with an I-told-you-so look and returned to the bar. Dad and Hollis returned to their conversation with the empty chairs. Although, thank goodness, they'd dropped the topic of Aunt Matilda's so-called murder. They seemed to be discussing what Edgar Allen Poe had been up to in the 150 or so years since his death.

And having a wonderful time. We'd probably be here gabbing until dawn. They would, at least. I was dog-tired from fighting traffic all the way out to the Eastern shore, and sick and tired of watching them pretend to talk to ghosts. Maybe I should skip the third margarita and find a quiet corner where I could take a nap.

But the margarita appeared beneath my nose while I was considering this idea, so I took a sip. This was the real thing again. I sighed with pleasure, closed my eyes, and leaned back in my chair.

"Look, this is all very interesting, but it's not going to solve Matilda's problem," a voice said. A male voice. But not Dad or Toby. Had someone else taken one of the empty chairs? I pondered whether it was worth the effort of opening my eyes to find out.

"You're right, Sam," said a voice. Perhaps I'd had enough margaritas; it really did sound like Aunt Matilda's voice.

"I really don't understand why she can't see us," Aunt Matilda was saying.

"Because you're not really there," I said opening my eyes.

They turned to stare at me. All four of them. Sam and Aunt Matilda were a little more transparent than Dad and Hollis, but I could actually see them. I recognized Aunt Matilda's bony angular frame and hawk nose. I was imagining Sam, of course, based on Hollis's descriptions of the handsome, spoiled rich boy who'd deserted her during their honeymoon and never been seen alive again. My imagination did a great job; I could see why Hollis fell for the louse.

Definitely enough margaritas. I shoved the glass away from me.

"I thought you said you couldn't see them," Hollis said.

"I can't see them. But I've been sitting here getting plastered, listening to you two talk to the air. Obviously I've started hallucinating them. Hi, Aunt Matilda. Sorry you're dead; you were less irritating than most of my aunts."

"Thanks, sweetie," Aunt Matilda said. "For a kid, you're okay, too. I'd have left you my money if I'd had any notion Aggie was going to knock me off and you'd be solving the case."

"Are you so sure there is a case?" I said.

"Well, that's what I've been trying to get them to tell you all evening," Aunt Matilda said.

"Maybe it loses a little in the translation," I said. "Try it again."

"All right," Aunt Matilda said. She leaned over to the ashtray where Hollis's cigarette was burning and inhaled deeply. The plume of smoke hovering over the ashtray drifted gently in her direction rather than rising straight up.

"Now why'd you go and do that?" Hollis grumbled. "You think I want it after you've been at it?"

"Well, light yourself one, then," Aunt Matilda said. "And another one for me, while I tell Meg about how she murdered me."

"Aunt Agatha, you mean," I said. "Why would she do that?"

"Wanted the house all to herself, of course," Aunt Matilda said. "Papa's will set it out that we both had the right to live in the house, and when one of us died, the survivor got the whole thing; lock, stock and barrel."

"Yes, but you've been living there together for over thirty years," I said. "Why would she suddenly decide to kill you?"

"Maybe she finally went off her rocker," Aunt Matilda said. "Who knows?"

"And no offense," I went on, "but you're both in your nineties; it isn't as if she's going to have a long time to enjoy her ill-gotten gains. And I would think that since she's been in the wheelchair, she's been glad to have you around."

"Yes, I expect she'll have to hire a home nurse now," Aunt Matilda said. "Serves her right."

Actually, come to think of it, Aunt Agatha would probably survive Aunt Matilda's departure rather well. She might be wheelchair-bound, but she still did most of the cooking, shopping, and cleaning; and found time to do volunteer work for several civic organizations.

In fact, I could see how Aunt Agatha might be relieved by Aunt Matilda's death. Having lost her husband to World War II and her son to the Korean War, Agatha had returned to her parents' house to nurse them through long, debilitating terminal illnesses. Most of the family thought her parents should have left the house to Agatha outright in recompense, and when Matilda moved in to claim her half, everyone had assumed it was only a brief stopover between husband #8 and whoever she had picked out as #9. Certainly no one expected her to stay for the next three decades, filling the house with cigarette smoke, empty bourbon bottles, loud music, and elderly but unsavory gentlemen callers.

Poor Aunt Agatha, I thought. No wonder she'd taken to tippling a little herself. Not that you could ever see the slightest sign of it, of course; she was much too ladylike. But when I'd gone over to help out, the morning after Aunt Matilda's death, I remembered how flustered she'd been when she realized that the drawer of her bedside table was open far enough to reveal a half-empty bourbon bottle. I'd popped the drawer closed before anything else could notice it. Aunt Agatha had always been a favorite of mine as well, for very different reasons. I'd always enjoyed going to their house to eat Aunt Agatha's fried chicken and chocolate pie while listening to Aunt Matilda's wild tales of her adventures in Las

Vegas and Tijuana. I couldn't imagine Aunt Agatha as a murderer.

"Okay," I said aloud. "Let's assume Aunt Agatha did have a motive for killing you. How did she do it?"

"She poisoned me." Aunt Matilda said, promptly.

"Dad, did they do a toxicology screen when Aunt Matilda died?" I asked.

"Of course," Dad said, pushing his glasses farther up his nose and assuming his professional doctor's expression. "And I made sure to see it. Nothing obviously suspicious; the only thing that showed up was the digitalis she was taking for her heart condition. They assumed she'd accidentally taken an overdose. Easy to do if you're absent-minded. But I should have guessed, of course; who knows how many heart patients are murdered with overdoses of their own medicine!"

"So you're saying Aunt Agatha killed you with an overdose of your own digitalis?"

"Yes," she said. "Clever really; Aggie was always a sneaky one. It was in the tea."

"How do you know?"

"Well, it had to be. I didn't eat or drink anything else. Except the cake, and we both had that. I cut the pieces, so there's no way she could have tampered with that."

"And she made the tea?"

"Well, no; I made the tea," Aunt Matilda said. "But I left the tray on her bedside table while I went back to get the cake plates. That must be when she did it."

"You made the tea? And fetched cake? Sounds unusual," I said.

"Well, I did it sometimes. When I wanted to be nice to her."

"When you wanted to weasel something out of her, more likely," I said. Aunt Matilda started to put on an indignant look, realized it wouldn't play to the present crowd, and settled for a shrug.

"Didn't usually get me anywhere," she said. "But worth trying."

"Any particular reason you were being nice to her that evening?" I asked.

"We'd had a big argument that day. I was trying to make it up to her."

"I remember hearing about that," Dad said. "You wanted to sell the house to that developer fellow. The one who needed either your land or the Walthams' to finish up his project."

"And Aggie wanted to squat there forever," Aunt Matilda said, with a sigh. "Well, I guess she's doing that now."

"Yes, when she wouldn't sell he went with the Walthams," Dad said. "Of course, he's wasting his money, either way; the planning commission will never approve a project like that when the town doesn't want it."

"Walthams made a mint from it, still," Aunt Matilda grumbled.

"Well, what do you care now," I said. "I mean, it is true about not being able to take it with you, isn't it?"

"Yes, but if it hadn't been for Aggie, I'd be back there enjoying all that loot, not sitting here in this dump. No offense," she said to Toby, who was replacing her apparently untouched margarita. Toby nodded, unoffended.

"Doesn't make sense," I said. "She didn't have to kill to keep you from selling the property. She owned half of it. All she had to do was refuse to sell."

"Well, tell that to Aggie," Matilda said. "I'm the one who ended up dead."

"Yes, and that's odd, isn't it," I said. "I mean, theoretically, you'd have a much stronger motive for murder than she does. All she had to do was refuse to sell. You'd have to either convince her to sell or knock her off to get what you wanted."

"I didn't say it made sense," Aunt Matilda said. "But it happened. I'm here, aren't I?"

"That's a matter of opinion," I said, glancing at my margarita.

"Is there anyone else who could have benefited from your death?" Hollis asked. "Agatha got the house, but who got the rest of your estate?"

"Well, most of it went to Meg's parents," Aunt Matilda said.

"And we were in Paris when you died," Dad said. "Which makes us rather unlikely suspects."

"You almost sound disappointed," Hollis said.

"He is," I muttered.

"But that's beside the point," Aunt Matilda said. "Don't waste your time on other possible suspects. Go after Aggie."

I took another sip of my margarita and suddenly, enlightenment struck. Either that or I suddenly reached that level of inebriation when every thought you have seems earth-shatteringly brilliant.

"You know one thing I've always admired about you, Aunt Matilda," I began.

"What's that?" she asked, frowning.

"Your honesty. I really admire the way you haven't actually told a lie tonight. You've tried to mislead us, but you haven't actually said, 'She put the digitalis in the tea.' All you said was, 'It was in the tea.' Of course it was; and you know that for sure because you put it there. And she guessed, and while you were out fetching the cake, she switched the cups."

"Impossible," Aunt Matilda said. "For one thing, I'd have noticed. She takes her tea black, while I take it with sugar. Two spoonfuls."

"And a stiff shot of bourbon; yes, I know," I said. "I wonder how long she'd been keeping that bourbon handy in her nightstand. The bottle was half-empty, so I doubt if it was the first time she'd added sugar and bourbon to her own tea and switched the cups. I wouldn't be surprised if she'd been doing it for years, every time you brought her tea, on the off chance that it might be the time you'd decided to poison her."

"Well, I never!" Aunt Matilda said.

"Meg, how can you sit there and accuse your own aunt of murder," Hollis put in.

I was about to point out that my aunt had accused her own sister of murder when Aunt Matilda spoke again.

"That conniving old bat! I thought it was a good joke, at first, that we'd both thought of the same thing the same night. But I knew something was up when I'd hung around the house for a couple of hours waiting for her to keel over too, and finally realized she wasn't going to."

"Matilda, you didn't," Dad said. "I'm disappointed in you!"

"Well, don't make a federal case of it," Matilda grumbled. "It certainly backfired on me, now, didn't it?"

Life, I thought, sipping my margarita, was inherently unfair. When I refused to follow in his footsteps and go to med school, Dad acted as if I'd committed an unspeakable crime; and now Aunt Matilda had just confessed to murder, and all he could say was that he was disappointed in her.

"Well, now that you know how she did it, I'm sure you can figure out some way to see she gets her comeuppance," Aunt Matilda said to me.

"Her comeuppance," I echoed. "You try to murder her, and she manages to kill you in self-defense, and you want me to frame her for your murder?"

"She didn't have to kill me," Aunt Matilda protested. "She could have just poured it out without drinking it."

"Yeah, and you didn't have to put digitalis in her tea to begin with."

"Well, I can't help that now," Aunt Matilda said. "Are you going to help bring my killer to justice?"

"Sorry," I said. "As far as I'm concerned, justice has already been done."

"Hmph," Aunt Matilda said. "Well, I see I left my money to the right parties after all."

With that, she vanished. We all looked at each other in silence for a few moments.

"Sorry," Sam said, finally. "I really believed her."

"So did I," Hollis said. "I should have known better."

"You had to know Matilda," Dad said.

"Yes," I added. "I'm sure none of your great aunts would do anything so underhanded."

"Are you kidding?" Hollis said, shaking her head. "That's exactly the sort of thing they'd all do. I just expected better from your family. Well, we'd better push off," she added, standing a trifle unsteadily and heading for the door. "Or we'll end up spending the night face down on Toby's floor."

"Yes, I suppose it is time," Dad said, knocking over a nearby chair as he stumbled after her.

"I'll drive you," Toby said, as he followed them out the door. "You're all three soused."

"All four," Sam chimed in. He winked as he floated gently out the door toward the parking lot, where I could hear Dad and Hollis both insisting that the other should ride in the dubious comfort of the truck cab.

I stood, braced myself against a chair, and focused my eyes to peer around the barroom. No translucent aunts anywhere.

"I'm sorry, Aunt Matilda," I said to the empty air. "I wish I could help you. But it was your own fault, you know."

No answer.

Toby stuck his head back in the door.

"You coming sometime this century?" he growled.

"Is she still here?" I said.

He stared at me for a few seconds, then ducked out the door again.

I looked around the room. Still no Aunt Matilda. But over in the corner of the bar, where one of the drunks was holding a cigarette, I could see the thin column of smoke flutter as if a breeze had stirred the room. A few seconds later, the drunk took a deep drag, then looked at the cigarette in disgust and stubbed it out.

"Bye, Aunt Matilda," I said, as I headed for the door. "Look me up sometime."

φφφ

Author's note: "Night Shades" is a collaboration of sorts. I've always loved (and envied) the world Helen Chappell created in her Hollis Ball mysteries set in the fictional Eastern Shore town of Oysterback, Maryland. And Helen has been saying for years that she'd love to meet my father, the inspiration for Meg's Dad. In this story, with Helen's permission, I take my characters to play for a few hours in her world. So I guess that makes Helen the unsung sixteenth contributor to this anthology.

φ

Like Meg Langslow, the ornamental blacksmith heroine of her series from St. Martin's Press, **Donna Andrews** was born and raised in Yorktown, Virginia. These days she spends almost as much time in cyberspace as Turing Hopper, the artificial intelligence who appears in her technocozy series from Berkley Prime Crime. *No Nest for the Wicket* (St. Martins, August 2006) is Andrews's eleventh book.

After graduating from the University of Virginia, where she majored in English and Drama with a concentration on writing, Andrews moved to the Washington, D.C. area and joined the communications staff of a large financial organization, where for two decades she honed her writing skills on nonfiction and developed a profound understanding of the criminal mind through her observation of interdepartmental politics.

A member of Mystery Writers of America, Sisters in Crime, and the Private Investigators and Security Association, Donna spends her free time gardening and conquering the world (but only in the computer game Civilization IV®).

GRAVE ENDS

by Elizabeth Foxwell

The child's body appeared again, this time on the tracks before her, his tiny arms held out like a reproach. She started forward to the edge of the platform, a thin, imperious figure in silk and cashmere.

"Aunt Lena?" Her great-niece Rachel moved to her side, sleek in snug black jeans and tight sweater. "What's the matter?"

"Are you blind, girl? Jump down and grab him before the train comes in!"

"Grab whom, Aunt?"

Lena looked again. The body was gone, vanished like blown smoke. Only a dark, muffled figure facing her on the platform—like the figure of Death.

"Are you all right, Aunt? You look pale. We can postpone the trip to the lawyer's."

"Of course I'm all right." She shook off Rachel's supporting arm but when the train arrived, she needed the conductor's strong hand around her veined one and an aft push from her great-niece to board. Stupid, she told herself, easing into a seat by a window. It had been so many years ago. Merely a figment, a trick of light on her old eyes, as it had been in her bedroom last night. Only a fancy that the vision had resembled Davey with his floppy black hair and funny big ears... She stared out of the window, her reflection showing not the firm, fair complexion and marcelled hairstyle of 75 years ago, but cords of sagging flesh and frustrated dreams.

The train started, moving slowly at first then gathering speed, trees and houses rushing together in a long blur. "Rachel—" She turned to her left, her niece's usual place, and frowned at the empty seat. Really, the flightiness of young people... She leaned over the armrest and saw Rachel down the aisle with a man in a tan trench coat, both examining a briefcase. How odd.

"Rachel!" Her tone was querulous, and Rachel came hurrying towards her, swinging the briefcase in a careless hand.

"What?"

"Who was that?" demanded Lena, squinting with rheumy eyes at the man hurrying away.

"No one special, Aunt." She set the briefcase on the seat across from Lena, her fingers moving swiftly over the latch.

"Is that his case?"

"Aren't you full of questions. No, it's mine."

"I don't remember it." She was still gazing down the aisle at the retreating figure. "He seems familiar." Something about the fuzzy shape of the ear—if only she could see more clearly.

"You're imagining things." Rachel's voice was abrupt. "Do you want a cup of tea?"

"No. The tea you bring is tepid, scalding or stewed." She leaned back in her seat and the images flickering past the window pushed her back to the past. "Rachel, did I ever tell you about Davey?"

Rachel exhaled. "The dead child. Yes, you have, Aunt. Several times."

"Strange; I thought…"

"I'm getting a soda." She stomped off. A film student, she had the young's hair-trigger leap to impatience. Like David, once upon a time, who had disliked the fuss of garters and foundation garments in the back seat of his father's Packard…

The withered reflection in the window smiled and closed possessive fingers around the triple circlet of pearls enclosing her bony neck—a gift from David. At opportune times he had been easy enough to manage, to persuade to part with some of his family's ill-gotten largess for something she wanted. Rachel herself would make a fine director some day, as she had handled her great-aunt's considerable finances with cool aplomb since last year, when she had moved into Lena's house to attend college. David had been a fine speakeasy manager but not a manager of a marriage nor of a child. No. Those had been singular weaknesses of his. But she had turned them into profit. After all, she had been unable to have children after Davey and was entitled to what solace money could buy.

In the window's reflection, something white flickered, like the folds of infant blankets. Her throat went dry.

"Here, lemonade." Rachel again, trying to push a Styrofoam cup into her clawed fingers. "You can't say that's too tepid."

She took it and lifted the cup to her lips. The baby reappeared, floating, before her, eyes bulging in his blue face. The cup dropped from her hand, splattering liquid across her lap, soaking into the expensive material like—like blood...

"Aunt? Are you ill?" Rachel's face weaved, strangers across the aisle turning hasty profiles from any prospect of a scene, and she turned back to the window. But the baby was still there.

"It wasn't my fault!" she cried, and stumbled into the aisle. Icy fingers pawed at her, a grasp from the grave, and she reeled onto the moving platform between the cars, clawing for air and succor. The bloated baby floated in front of her eyes, holding out his arms. The door seemed to yawn into a writhing darkness, ground rushing beneath her. And the shove between her thin shoulder blades and the vicious wrench at her throat, she knew, was David's summons to join him in the next world.

φ

The police met the train at the next stop, one of those grassy, deserted stations that dotted the countryside, and questioned the dead woman's great-niece who had her face buried in her handkerchief, and a dark-haired man in a suavely tailored suit who identified himself as the deceased's attorney. While the girl sobbed, the lawyer talked gravely of the deceased's frailty of mind that had led to the fatal leap from the train. Eventually the train chugged on to its next destination, and the police and the conductor, lulled by the simple explanation that involved neither complex investigation nor negligence for the railroad, disappeared up the line in mutual accord to examine the spot where the deceased had fallen and remove the body.

Rachel lowered the handkerchief, revealing perfectly dry eyes. "Have they gone?"

Tossing a tan trench coat over his arm, the lawyer wandered to the end of the empty platform, kicking loose pebbles, and peered down the line. "Yes."

"Good." She lit a cigarette and followed him. "I thought we'd just have reason to commit her. Never anticipated this lucky break. Good riddance." She took a deep, virtuous drag. "The time I spent fetching and carrying for that old bat, and all the while—you said—she was planning to rewrite her will and cut me out! The nerve. Fixing up that film with the dead brat's photograph and rigging the briefcase was a cinch." Rachel puffed energetically. "She lost it at the end, babbling about it not being her fault, whatever the hell that means. The film must have sent her over the edge."

He prodded the uneven edge of the platform with a thoughtful toe. "Impossible."

She pulled the pearl choker from her pocket, gloating over its twisted remains, then paused, cocking her head at him. "What do you mean?"

"I mean—the camera jammed after the first run-through outside the train. It wasn't working."

The smoke from her cigarette seemed to hang in the air. A train whistle sounded in the near distance and he glanced casually toward it. "But it was kind of you to eliminate a millstone around my family's neck."

She stared at him, he with his floppy black hair and odd large ears, and he laughed.

"Where did you think her money came from? The lottery? Don't be naive. After I tracked her down, I persuaded your sainted aunt that the money should revert to Grandfather's blood heir. So wise, avoiding those distasteful charges of blackmail. I also persuaded her to sign the will before her grasping great-niece had—other ideas. She was just coming to fetch her copy."

She fell back a step, her wide eyes mesmerized by the speed of the approaching train and his looming form, and he slid the pearls adroitly from her numb fingers.

"Nice to have these back. And I do so appreciate your saving me from messing about with dreary poisons or pills. So tedious and time-consuming."

His well-placed push sent Rachel to join her great-aunt, right where the shabby platform crumbled into broken stone. He, who would speak smoothly of a great-niece's grief and careless footing and display the bleeding nails of a too-tardy swipe to save her, was a good manager too.

And he thought he heard a child's cry mingled in the shriek of the whistle.

φφφ

Elizabeth Foxwell has published nine short stories. Her World War I-set short story "No Man's Land" won the Agatha Award and was nominated for a Macavity Award; it appears in *World's Finest Mystery and Crime Stories* (Tor, 2004) and *Blood on Their Hands* (Berkley, 2003). She edited the Malice Domestic serial novel *The Sunken Sailor* (Berkley, 2004) and coauthored *The Robert B. Parker Companion* (Berkley, 2005). Foxwell hosts a weekly radio program, "It's a Mystery," on WEBR in Fairfax, VA.

BEACH, BOARDWALK AND MURDER
by Mary Ellen Hughes

Maggie leaned back on her blanket and raised her face to the sun. Ahh, pure pleasure. She dug her toes into the warm sand and took a deep breath of the fresh, salty air. Ocean City, Maryland, that tourist trap of T-shirt shops and greasy boardwalk fries seemed like Shangri-La after nine months of teaching math at McHenry High in Baltimore. No sleepy-eyed students, no painfully illogical test papers, no parents, no principal.

She sat up suddenly with a jerk and fumbled through her large tote, searching for a familiar shape. Shoot! No sun screen either. Now what?

It had taken her forever to park the car and lug all her stuff down the beach, searching for the perfect spot to plant herself—away from screeching toddlers and booming tape players. Should she leave it all here for the time it would take her to find a shop selling sun screen? She'd have to.

Grumbling, Maggie picked up her wallet and took a speculative glance at the rest of her possessions. All replaceable, she decided, if they somehow walked away during her absence. But hey, she chided herself, this was the beach! No one lazing here in the sun could possibly have the energy or evil inclination towards thievery.

She'd been living in the city too long—two years now. And teaching in a city high school where, unfortunately, one never left one's pocketbook in an unlocked drawer. Her attitude needed to change here, at Ocean City, where all things negative were left behind, and only things pleasant, calming and good were allowed. Or so she told herself, and was just about convinced.

When Maggie came back, after an inexplicably long search through too many shops, she noticed newcomers near her blanket. They were an acceptable distance away, and they looked like a quiet, middle-aged couple, so Maggie barely gave them a thought before settling down and slathering herself up with her not-very-reasonably-priced sunburn protection. Maggie's fair skin and blue eyes, and too many painful burns growing up, had made her careful.

A pair of college-aged men-on-the-prowl strolled slowly in front of her, looking her over with interested eyes, pausing casually as they waited for an inviting signal from her. Forget it, Maggie flashed, telepathically. You're about five years too young, and I'm about five minutes away from a vegetative state. She rolled onto her stomach, smoothed the sand out under her Daffy Duck beach blanket, and laid her head down for her first beach nap of the season.

She didn't know how long she had slept, or if she really had slept, but low voices gradually crept into her consciousness.

"How much does he want to do it?"

"We haven't discussed that yet."

"Don't let him ask for too much. She's old. I heard they charge more for young ones."

"Be quiet. We shouldn't even be talking about it here. Hand me a beer."

"They don't allow beer on the beach. They're giving fines now."

"Oh for cryin' out... Fines for beer you're worried about, but not... Gimme something cold."

Maggie's eye, the one, that is, not pressed against her blanket and that was facing away from the voices, had popped open at about the tenth word. Sleep immediately fled, and her mind raced over what she had just overheard.

She waited for what would come next, but the conversation became innocuous: Where do you want to eat later? There's a good movie playing. Are you going in the water?

Maggie forced herself to stay quiet, feigning sleep until the speakers gradually lapsed into silence. Waiting longer still, she slowly began to move, stretching as if just waking up, and rolled onto her back. Her gaze aimed in every direction except the speakers', until finally, with some elaborately casual fumbling and shifting, she glanced over at their blanket.

The woman was middle-aged, possibly fifty, and wore a black skirted swimsuit over a well-fed figure. A white turban covered all but a few wisps of light brown hair. The man was probably the same age, pot-bellied and balding.

Maggie had to strain to keep from staring with her mouth open. Had these two actually said what she heard? They looked like a mom and pop that might have run the deli down the street from her apartment. 'Whatcha want, darlin', turkey with mayo on wheat?' would be what she expected to hear from them, not, 'How much? She's old.' Maybe she hadn't heard quite right?

But then she noticed the eyes. Both had hard, steely eyes. Not the kind you'd want to see looking down at you as you lay helpless, say, in an emergency room. But still, was she putting more into what she had heard than she should? What if she wasn't? What should she do?

Maggie struggled with that thought for a long time, unable now to relax, not even seeing the ocean in front of her or caring about the sun beating down on her. It occurred to her she could just forget about it, pretend she hadn't heard anything at all, and go on with her vacation. But that went against her nature, her total self. Maybe it had something to do with her math training, she didn't know. But she couldn't leave something hanging, unsolved, not dealt with. It would be impossible for her to ignore it.

Maggie became aware that the pair were packing up their things, preparing to leave. She watched until they had walked to the edge of the sand, where the beach grass started sprouting, then saw them turn into the patio area of the hotel there.

Before she thought about what she was doing Maggie jumped up and ran across the beach to the patio. She paused beside a large tree, and was just in time to see them disappear into the hotel's back door. Maggie scurried up to the door, peeked in, and saw them turning a corner at the end of the hall. A dash down the hall got her there in time to see the elevator doors closing in front of the couple. She watched the light shift on the numbers above the door and pause on four.

Maggie scurried back out to the patio area. She sat down in a vinyl-strapped chair, puffing for breath by now, and gazed up at the balconies. What if they don't have an ocean view room, she worried? Most of the balconies were empty, but scanning the row on the fourth level, Maggie stopped at one with an elderly woman sitting on it, wearing a long orange caftan and a shawl of some sort over her shoulders. As Maggie watched, the black-suited, white turbaned woman stepped through the sliding door and leaned over the older woman. Bingo!

So now she knew where they were staying. But she didn't know their names, and she didn't really know if they were planning the deadly deed that her imagination had put together from the few words she had overheard. She didn't know if they were hiring a hit man to do away with that sweet old woman up there.

Maggie didn't sleep well that night. When she did manage to drop off, she kept dreaming of orange caftaned bodies being dropped off the ends of piers with cement blocks tied to their feet. Not exactly sweet dreams.

As she lay in bed, in her budget-priced motel room two blocks off the ocean, having finally given up on trying to get any rest, she thought about what she would do. It was flimsy, but it was the best she could come up with so far. After all, she was a math teacher, not Sam Spade, private eye. She doubted that even Sam would have any great ideas, considering the circumstances.

That morning, she hung around the beach area just outside the hotel where the tawdry twosome were staying. She could just see the pool through the neatly trimmed tree branches, and she waited with fluctuating hopes. If "granny" wasn't a pool-sitter, Maggie was out of luck.

Just as she had deflected her twenty-third curious glance from a passer-by, Maggie saw what she was waiting for. The orange-caftaned old lady came walking somewhat unsteadily on the arm of a white-turbaned younger woman, today wearing a lime green cover-up over her black bathing suit. The pair headed into the fenced pool area, and settled, with some fussing and fumbling, into two blue vinyl-strapped lounge chairs. Maggie felt like cheering. Instead, she silently pumped her fist and hissed a "yes!", grinning at the little boy walking by who looked up at her with startled eyes.

Maggie waited until the pool attendant became engrossed in something at the far end, away from the gate, then casually slipped in and took a lounge chair one down from granny. It helped that a group of noisy children with their parents followed soon after, and Maggie felt she blended in unnoticed despite being a trespasser.

She leaned back in her chair and half-closed her eyes pretending to mind her own business, while her ears practically turned like radar dishes to pick up everything they could from the two women nearby.

"Auntie, aren't you a little too warm with that robe on?"

So it was Auntie, not granny.

"Leave me alone. I'm still capable of judging my own temperature."

"Of course you are, Auntie. I just…"

"Just shut up. And if you can't, get the hell out of here."

"Now…" The turbaned woman snapped her mouth shut as Auntie gave her a glare that could melt the plastic earrings off her earlobes.

Well. Change "granny" to "auntie", and "sweet old lady" to just "old lady". Maybe there was a good reason for knocking her off after all. Maggie started to chuckle then instantly felt guilty. Even disagreeable people had the right to live out their lives, didn't they?

The pair were quiet for a while, then the younger woman got fidgety.

"Auntie, would you like something to eat or drink? I'm a bit hungry myself."

"Good Lord, Carla, you ate enough for two at breakfast. What more could you possibly want?"

"Just a bite. Something sweet. Anything for you?"

"No, no. Go feed your face. You might as well look at the bathing suits in the shop here, while you're at it. You'll be needing the next size up before long."

Carla's face flushed pink but she managed a stiff smile. She zipped up her lime green cover-up, slipped into her flip-flops and left. Auntie's face took on a satisfied look. She reached into the bag beside her and pulled out a large square of yellow and green crocheting attached to a crochet hook and two balls of yarn, and began to work at it furiously. Maggie watched the woman's fingers fly in fascination, and her gaze apparently caught Auntie's attention, for the older woman looked over sourly at her.

"My Gran used to make something like that," Maggie said, which happened to be true. "I forget what she called it."

"Leaf cluster."

"Yes! She was always going to teach me how to do it, but never got around to it."

"Died?"

"Yes."

"Mmmf."

Auntie was silent for a while, working her stitches, then she glared over at Maggie who still watched.

"Don't expect me to offer to teach you this. I can't be bothered. You can go pay some yarn shop if you want to learn it."

"No, I just enjoy watching. You know, I remember reading about a group of women somewhere during World War II who knitted coded messages into their stuff to smuggle information across enemy lines."

Auntie looked over her half glasses. "Must have been some ugly sweaters."

Maggie laughed. "Maybe so. Maybe that made them easier to smuggle out. The enemy was glad to see them go."

Auntie snorted, and the edges of her mouth turned up a tiny bit. "How'd they send the answers back? Argyle socks?"

"I don't know. Maybe they dropped cross-stitched tea cozies from airplanes."

Auntie really snorted now, and had to reach into a pocket for a handkerchief.

Maggie looked up and saw Carla approaching. She was munching on a Danish and frowning in Maggie's direction.

"Listen," Maggie said, in a lowered tone to Auntie, "I've got to talk to you alone. I think you may be in danger."

The old woman looked at her and didn't answer.

She probably thinks I'm crazy, Maggie thought.

Carla came into the pool area and sat down on the other side of her aunt. She began to say something but the older woman interrupted her in mid-sentence.

"I've had enough sun now, Carla. I'm going back to the room."

"Oh! Of course." Carla began slipping her toes back into her flip-flops.

"No, you stay here."

"But…"

"This young lady will take me up. I'm going to teach her how to crochet."

Maggie swallowed her surprise and smiled sweetly at Carla, whose steely eyes formed daggers. Maggie ignored the evil looks and helped Auntie gather her things and head back to the hotel.

"Tell Earl to leave us alone too," Auntie tossed over her shoulder to Carla. "I don't need him blaring the T.V."

"Earl went to Salisbury, Auntie."

"Good. I hope he stays there."

Maggie and Auntie made their way up to the fourth floor and to room 418. Inside the room, which was actually a suite with living room, kitchenette and two bedrooms, the old woman dropped her bag and sank onto the couch, pointing to a chair for Maggie.

"Name's Florence Lang. You can call me Flo."

"Hi Flo. I'm Maggie Olenski."

"Well, we're alone. What's this all about."

Maggie told her what she had overheard on the beach. Flo listened quietly, her only comment being, "Hmpf."

"I could be wrong," Maggie said, "but it sounded to me as though Carla and Earl want to hire someone to kill you."

"They'd have to hire someone. They're too stupid to do it themselves."

"So you think I'm right?"

"Hmpf." Maggie took that as a yes.

"I think we should call the police."

"No!"

Maggie was surprised at Flo's vehemence.

"You don't want the police?"

"No. They'll talk to my niece and her husband who will just tell them I'm a crazy old woman and that you misunderstood them. Then Carla and Earl will know I know and they'll be extra cautious. But it won't stop them. Believe me, it won't stop them."

"But we have to do something."

Flo was quiet for a while, staring out the window at the ocean.

"Maybe you could help me?" she said. It was said in her usual gruff tone, but Maggie heard the plaintiveness underneath. Suddenly Flo was Maggie's old Gran with her leaf cluster afghan and trembling chin. How could she refuse?

"Of course, if I can."

They talked for a while, throwing out ideas and picking them apart, finally coming up with what seemed like a reasonable plan. At least Maggie hoped it was reasonable. She had never had to prevent a murder before, so how did she know what would work and what wouldn't? She wished Flo would agree to bringing in the police, but could understand the argument against it. If they didn't believe her, it might just be postponing her death. They would have to stop it now.

"By the way," Maggie said, "I assume they are doing this for money?"

"What else? They're my only heirs. I've never written up a will. The thought always gave me the chills, like digging my own grave."

Maggie suddenly looked toward the door. She thought she heard Carla flip-flopping down the hall and quickly grabbed the crochet bag. In a moment a key rattled in the lock, and Flo's not-so-loving niece walked in to see Maggie twisting yarn around the hook in a way that any experienced needlewoman would know was insane, but Carla only looked away disinterestedly.

"Auntie, remember we're meeting Earl at the Peking Palace for lunch. He *has* to have Chinese food." She rolled her eyes. "He's got this craving now for it. He hasn't had it for so long because you know how it can bother him. He told them, though, when he called for reservations, not to put any MSG in his order. That man drives me absolutely crazy with his cravings." She sank into a chair, having dropped towels and tote bags along the way. "He's got to have *what* he wants *when* he wants it. Like that power drill last fall. He had to have it, but does he ever use it now? And that..." Remembering her manners she suddenly turned to Maggie. "Would you like to join us for lunch, Miss uh...?" Carla gave Maggie a shark-like smile.

"Olenski. Maggie. No, thank you. I've really got to run. Thanks Flo. I'm going to work on this."

Flo said, "Hmpf," and Maggie dashed out, crossing her fingers that what she and Flo had discussed would be enough.

That evening, Maggie got a call from Flo.

"They're going up to Atlantic City tomorrow, meeting friends and staying the night."

"Ah, the alibi. Anything else?"

"Just that Earl was real edgy at lunch today, and ever since. Carla's been fussing over me like I was a Ming vase."

"When are they leaving?"

"Sometime in the afternoon. Say they don't want to leave me alone too long. Hah!"

"Did they suggest you stay in the room while they're gone?"

"Oh yes. They don't want me out of reach, do they? They've loaded up on food for me, and some to take with them for the drive. I told them I'd make them chicken salad for sandwiches if they got me the ingredients. I like to be busy. Keeps my mind off nasty thoughts. Lord, you'd a thought I was fixing them caviar and champagne the way Carla carried on. She's playing it to the hilt. I'll be glad when they're gone."

Yes, Maggie thought, but what will happen then?

φ

The next afternoon Maggie stood near the hotel parking lot under a leafy tree, waiting to see Earl and Carla pack up their car. The night before, she had called her younger brother Joe in Baltimore. Joe had a summer job in a lawyer's office, and she asked him to find out a few things for her if he could. He returned her call late this morning. What he told her gave Maggie much food for thought.

Suddenly Flo's niece and her husband came out of the side door of the hotel, laden with luggage and a blue cooler. Earl wore shorts and a loud, flower-printed shirt, and Carla was minus her white turban for a change, her hair looking freshly curled. She wore an aqua top over tight white pants.

Maggie watched as they stowed their things. They climbed into opposite sides of the car, and Earl turned the ignition. Maggie stepped out from her hiding place and walked across their path, doing her best imitation of a double take as she glanced over at them.

"Why, hello! Are you leaving?" She craned her neck as if looking for Flo in the back seat.

Carla gave one of her frightening smiles. "No, we're just going up to Atlantic City for the night. Auntie is staying here."

"Oh, wow! Atlantic City. That sounds great. You know, I have a cousin that works a blackjack table at the Crystal Palace. Is that where you're staying?"

Carla tossed her head with a casual smugness. "No, we'll be at the Taj Mahal."

"I heard it's great there. Really nice. Well, have a good time."

Maggie stepped back, and the car pulled away from her. Carla looked back and Maggie sauntered towards the beach, as if that were where she had been heading all along. When they were out of sight, and too long gone to want to run back for any forgotten items, Maggie doubled back and dashed into the hotel, taking the elevator to Flo's room.

"They're gone," Flo said as she opened the door.

"I know. I saw them leave."

"Thought they'd never go. Earl drove me crazy with his damned nervous pacing, jingling the change in his pockets until I could have kicked him. And Carla simpering about how they hated to leave me. Hah! I knew what was really on their minds, and they're in for a surprise, aren't they?"

"Yes," Maggie said, but she had Joe's call on her mind. It was still bothering her. She sniffed the air, identifying freshly chopped onion among other things, and looked over to the kitchenette area. "Got any of that chicken salad left?"

"You hungry? Carla and Earl took it all. I was going to fix something for dinner later. Want me to do it now?"

"No, I'll just munch on this." Maggie pulled at a banana in the fruit bowl. It was attached to another one which knocked over a small jar behind the bowl as it came out. She righted the jar and lined it up with the other spices in the wall rack nearby, squeezing the "Accent" in next to the "Basil". Maggie sat down on the couch, but Flo continued to stand, fidgeting with the things on the counter, folding and refolding the hand towel, opening cabinets, putting things in, then pulling them back out.

"If it's too hard on you to stay here, we could go with plan B and spend the night at my room," Maggie said, watching Flo's nervous movements.

"No, I'm all right. Just keyed up. Maybe I'll work on my afghan. It's the waiting that's so hard. I'm sure nothing will happen until nighttime."

"No, I don't expect so."

Flo grabbed her crocheting and Maggie watched as her fingers flew again, fascinated to see the pattern grow. It's amazing, she thought, how a small action can produce such a complex result, eventually. Yes, a small action.

Maggie looked thoughtfully over at the kitchen area. A tiny frown formed at her brow.

"How long a drive is it to Atlantic City?" Maggie asked.

"They said they'd be there by six, so about three hours."

"Mmm. So they'll eat your sandwiches in the car, as they drive, I suppose."

Flo looked at Maggie over her glasses. Her fingers never missed a stitch. "I suppose," she said.

Maggie remembered the World War II knitters, and wondered what Flo's stitches would say right now if you could read them.

"I spoke to my brother Joe a little while ago. He works in a lawyer's office in Baltimore. They know how to find out lots of things."

"Do they?"

"Yes. He found out what may be a motive for Carla and Earl."

"Oh?"

"It seems a cousin of yours recently passed away, Flo. A rather wealthy cousin. Did you know that?" Maggie didn't wait for an answer. "She didn't leave a will, so all her money automatically goes to her two surviving relatives—Carla and you."

"That so? I thought Carla and Earl were my only relatives."

"So you told me. The thing is, the fewer surviving relatives there are, the less the money is divided."

"Hmpf."

"So getting rid of you would give Carla and Earl a nice chunk of money."

"Hmpf."

"But then, it also goes the other way around, doesn't it? Getting rid of Carla and Earl would give *you* a nice chunk of money, wouldn't it?"

Flo's needle stopped. She didn't look over at Maggie.

"Did you put something in those sandwiches, Flo? Maybe a lot of Accent, for flavoring, which happens to be mostly MSG? Monosodium Glutamate? Earl is allergic to MSG. Carla mentioned that yesterday. Maybe he's allergic enough to have a devastating reaction, perhaps while he's driving, possibly causing a fatal accident on a busy highway?"

Flo put down her leaf cluster afghan. She stared at it silently for a long time.

"I'm not rich," she said so softly Maggie had to strain to hear her. "I have no will because there'd be nothing left by the time I died. Carla and Earl have been stuck with me, and I've been stuck with them. Half of that inheritance wasn't good enough. I need enough to be independent. I could hire someone to take care of me, someone I could put up with, and live a good life for the years I have left. Was that too much to ask?"

"It is if murder is part of the answer."

"But they would have murdered *me*."

Maggie just looked at Flo. This was a family? Were homicidal tendencies a part of their DNA, passed down like red hair in some families, or long earlobes, or color blindness?

"You have to stop it, Flo."

Flo looked up with tired, resigned eyes. "How?"

"They have a cell phone. I saw it. You must have the number. You have to call them and warn them about the chicken salad."

Flo gave a long, deep sigh. "Yes, I suppose I have to." She pulled herself out of the couch, groaning with stiffness, and walked over to the telephone. Maggie watched her, and listened to her side of the conversation. She could only imagine what sort of reaction was going on in the car that was speeding its way to Atlantic City.

What would Flo do now, she wondered? This didn't end her problems with Carla and Earl, but only escalated them. Maggie could take her out of this hotel, out of their reach for now, but she had to live somewhere. Maggie knew there was help for senior citizens of limited means to move into retirement centers. Maybe she should suggest that to Flo. But then she thought about the other residents. What if Flo took a strong dislike to any of them? Then what?

Maggie sighed, and walked over to the window. She looked out at the waves rolling softly against the beach. Ocean City, she thought, where all things negative were left behind, and only good and pleasant things were allowed. Right, and the boardwalk fries were fat-free and all the T-shirts were Made in USA.

She heard Flo put down the phone. Maggie said, still looking out at the water, "Next year I think I'll probably go to the mountains for my vacation."

There was no response for a few moments. Then Maggie heard, "Hmpf."

φφφ

Mary Ellen Hughes is the author of *Wreath of Deception* (Berkley, 2006) the first of her new Craft Corner mystery series, with the second book, *String of Lies*, due out in September, 2007. "Beach, Boardwalk and Murder" features the protagonist of her first two novels, *A Taste of Death* and *Resort to Murder* (Avalon). Her short stories have also appeared in various mystery magazines.

Mary Ellen lives with her husband, Terry, in Maryland where most of her novels are set, though as a Wisconsin native she hopes to eventually give that state equal time. When not writing, she enjoys dabbling in various crafts such as beading and wreath-making, or sports such as tennis or skiing.

SISTER MARGARETE
by Betty Hyland

The faint sliver of new moon still hung in the dark sky as the first beams of the morning sun shone on the mossy, stone buildings of the Convent of Saint Dominic of San Sisto on the far eastern tip of Long Island. Curious seagulls flew inland from the Atlantic ocean as Matins, the early morning prayer service in the chapel, ended and the thirty or so members of the religious community prepared to start their day. Sister Margarete emerged through the heavy cedar doors first, her pleasant round face bent, her expression intense, as she hurried as best she could along the brick pathway to her room in the infirmary.

Ordinarily, she would go directly to the gathering place with the other sisters to share breakfast from the communal bowls and platters. But today she had something to write down before it slipped from her dim memory so she walked quickly but carefully, gripping her cane with her large, red hand, her long wooden rosary beads clacking against her habit.

Her mind teemed with a story that had come to her during Matins when she saw a mouse dart across the chapel floor. As she watched the frightened creature zigzag behind the marble altar, the story interrupted her chanting so insistently she had been startled by its vividness. She was anxious to write the story down before it returned to that chamber of her brain where it had been hidden for so many years. *How many years?* she wondered, as she paused to catch her breath by the heavy door to the infirmary in the rear of the convent. *At least as many as seventy,* she thought. That's right. She must have been no more than an eight year old girl at the time. Holding tight to each thought as it came to her, Sister Margarete went directly to her small room on the first floor, wound a sheet of paper into her typewriter and began:

I saw a mouse in the chapel today. As it zigzagged away from me, I thought of my Uncle Earl's farmhouse in upstate New York. Mice were everywhere in the old brick house in those Depression days before the Second World War.

Good start, thought Margarete. I've got who, where and when. Miss Clarkson will be proud. Miss Clarkson was a retired English teacher from Montauk Point who was helping some of the older sisters in the infirmary write stories about their youth, most particularly their vocation stories. Something must have jarred the remembrance part of my brain, thought Margarete, because I haven't thought about that house in years. Nor those mice. Nor, God love him, Uncle Earl.

She gazed out her window through the branches of a white dogwood tree to the sprawling convent grounds beyond, took a deep breath and went on:

Uncle Earl had mousetraps set with what he called 'rat cheese,' a sharp cheddar, in the cellar, pantry, shed and behind the kerosene stove. Sometimes, in the middle of the night, a trap would go off. 'Got him!' he would thunder, and roar down the stairs to view his spoil like Ernest Hemingway viewing a felled water buffalo.

Sister Margarete had always worked with her hands, digging, planting, harvesting the gardens that fed the convent community. She loved the feel of wet earth, the smell of tomato plants, the cawing of crows. She loved being outside under the beautiful, changing skies.

In all her long years as a Dominican nun—she was a novice of eighteen when she joined—it had never occurred to her to write, never knew she would know how. Didn't you have to have a college degree, at least, to qualify as a writer? Suddenly she was excited about this story, anxious to see where it was going. Miss Clarkson might like the writing. It was vivid. Had a sense of place. And time. Pleased with herself, Margarete typed on:

I have a special memory of a breakfast Uncle Earl and I shared early one morning when I was about eight. Aunt Delia was long gone so it was just the two of us in the house.

I was sitting at the kitchen table in a flannel nightgown.

Uncle Earl was standing at the kerosene stove stirring a pot of cornmeal and singing out "The Man on the Flying Trapeze." Suddenly, he shouted, "Son of a gun!" and slammed down the pot.

Margarete leaned back, grinning, remembering Uncle Earl's salty tongue, his booming voice. Memories were tumbling out now.

A small field mouse had darted from behind the stove and skittered across the linoleum. It fled down the cellar stairs with Uncle Earl after it, and me flying right behind him. He grabbed a flashlight and, after a cobwebby search, we spotted her beside the warm coal furnace. Uncle Earl put his arm around me as we gazed at her over the back of the old busted couch.

Margarete now clearly recalled the tiny family scene.

The mouse lay on her side in a fluffy nest of dust, nursing her five babies. They were pink, not a speck of hair on them, and their eyes were closed. They were about as big as dimes.

"Can I put them in my room?" I whispered.

"No!" Uncle Earl had a stunned expression on his face.

"I could put milk in my Dydee doll's bottle," I pleaded.

The Dydee doll may give an historical touch, thought Margarete, remembering the popular baby doll that drank from a little bottle and wet its diaper. Miss Clarkson often stressed specificity.

Uncle Earl and Aunt Delia had never had children, so never felt easy around them, didn't know how to talk to them. He would rather stop by the saloon near the railroad station to throw darts and have a couple of "pick me ups"— slang for shots of whiskey—than read a nursery rhyme. Easy talk about politics or fishing came more naturally to him.

"Their mother knows how best to take care of them," he said.

"I could feed the mother some of my food. Then, she wouldn't have to go in the flour bin or bread box."

I pictured the five baby mice asleep in a row like my Dionne quintuplet dolls. They were girl mice, I was certain, and I named them Marie, Yvonne, Emily, Annette, and Cecile after the quints that had been born in Canada.

"They're best left alone," said Uncle Earl, lifting me into his arms.

I went back later in the morning to see the mice, but they were gone. When I asked Uncle Earl where he thought they were, he said the mother had probably moved them to a better hiding place.

I believed him.

I still do.

THE END

Margarete slipped the story in a folder, planning to read it to the class Tuesday when Miss Clarkson came to the infirmary. There were nine other sisters in the class. Miss Clarkson was helping them write down childhood memories which were to be presented to Sister Angela, the convent historian, at Christmas.

Angela had thought the personal accounts— not necessarily just of their vocations—would enrich the ongoing history of their religious community which went back several hundred years. The archives held wonderful stories, pictures, letters of the early nuns who had come over from the Mother House in Prouille, Italy, to found this convent, but there was little written recently, not in this age of television and computers.

Tuesday came and went but Margarete had not had a chance to read her story about Uncle Earl because Miss Clarkson took a good bit of time explaining point of view and how to handle flashbacks. Also several of the other sisters in the infirmary had shared their personal vocation stories which had been read aloud and discussed. Margarete's wasn't a true vocation story. She couldn't remember a time when she hadn't wanted to be a nun. When she turned eighteen, she had simply taken a bus to the convent, walked in the front gate and never looked back.

Even though she knew her story about mice at Uncle Earl's farmhouse was just a simple childhood remembrance, Margarete found herself thinking about it more than she expected. For example, last Wednesday, when the Angelus bell rang at noon, she had stopped to pray while on the path to the grotto when, out of the blue, something flashed into her mind as though a picture had been popped in front of her eyes. The picture was so startling, she had rested on the wooden bench facing the statue of Mary as a different, clearer picture emerged of the farmhouse.

Those cellar stairs were winding and narrow. You had to hold onto the walls to get down, even sideways. Canned goods, pails, and mops, burlap bags of potatoes and turnips, crocks of sauerkraut and vinegar beets lined the sides. How could she and Uncle Earl have clattered down them after that mouse? Uncle Earl always had to carry her down.

When her heart had stopped pounding from the exertion of the walk from the grotto and from the intensity of the memory, Margarete returned to her room and by the light of her window, reread her story. No sense changing it. Miss Clarkson would probably tell her it would slow down the action to describe the staircase, and it wouldn't change the story. This was really an exercise in memory expansion, anyway, something for Sister Angela's history files.

Even now, in the quiet of her room, she remembered how much she loved Uncle Earl, how good he had been to her. She had plenty of other memories she could write about—for example, how he took her on trolley car rides and bought her vanilla bean ice cream cones when she was a good little girl. But the story about the mice seemed particularly warm and vivid. She wouldn't change it.

Sister Margarete gazed out across the convent grounds remembering summers on Uncle Earl's farm—the stands of corn and the raspberry hedges, a favorite hydrangea bush, a wine glass elm. Her father had been a grammar school teacher and her mother worked in a toy factory to supplement their income. Those were the Depression years, after all. Most summers, she was sent to Uncle Earl's to be away from the boiling heat and dangerous streets of New York City. His farm was just a few miles north, in Duchess County.

Margarete loved telling Uncle Earl stories. Just the other day she told the writing group about his recipe for mustard, which was dry mustard, black pepper, fresh grated horseradish and a shot of that awful smelling whiskey from the pick-me-up bottle he kept behind the icebox. "Cures what ails you," he used to bellow when he took a swig right from the bottle, wiping his mouth on the sleeve of his shirt. Salty old Uncle Earl!

Sitting at her desk, now, with the morning sun shining on her starched white veil, her hands clasped together prayer-like in her lap, Margarete pictured those cellar stairs again. Hadn't a crock of that mustard been kept there? No wonder she had to be carried down. She probably would have smashed everything to smithereens, a clumsy girl like she had been, big for her age and overweight.

She pushed the folder to the back of the desk and returned to the window. She probably kept picturing those cellar stairs because she knew what really happened about those mice…not what she had written. She realized she had changed the story a little to make it a cute memory to give to Sister Angela. But it wasn't true. Not quite. Funny how she changed it! She returned to the desk and typed on a fresh piece of paper:

What happened after we found the mice was Uncle Earl raced upstairs for the tea kettle, then poured boiling water all over the mouse and her babies until they shriveled. When I started to cry, my screaming must have startled him so bad he accidentally splashed boiling water on my stomach and down my leg making these shiny, puckered marks you can still see right here underneath my habit.

"It was a true accident," Uncle Earl told Mother later. "I felt so responsible I smeared bacon fat on her right away."

"Don't feel bad. Her screaming could wake the dead," Mother had told him. She soaked me in Epsom salts baths which felt soothing but never did make the skin right.

Sister Margarete bunched the folds of her habit over the shiny, puckered spots hidden beneath, folded the sheet of paper in quarters and put it in her pocket. Although she didn't intend to alter the original story, she felt a need to write thoughts which now poured from her memory like a waterfall.

She took out a fresh sheet of paper:

Aunt Delia left before I was three, but I knew she was called a Flapper because she rouged her knees in a flirty way, wore glittery jewelry, and bobbed her hair.

Whenever I asked Mother where Delia had gone, she always said, "One day, she just walked out on your poor Uncle Earl. Told him she was going to New Orleans."

"So sudden?"

"Just sashayed out, leaving half her belongings, wearing that glittery jewelry. Good riddance to bad rubbish," Mother had sympathized with Uncle Earl, "leaving you high and dry like that. Just common downtown trash. Hope she's dead."

Aunt Delia never came back.

Sister Margarete went to the small one-burner unit in the corner of her room to boil water, but then couldn't remember where the teabags were. She felt as if the part of her brain behind her forehead had twisted like a snarled movie film. Holding her empty teacup in both hands, she stood in the middle of the floor, trying to recall a memory more than seventy years old. Suddenly, a very clear picture burst into her mind and she hurried to her typewriter. Uncle Earl's voice had boomed out so clearly, she heard him in the room and shivered. She wrote:

Sometimes Uncle Earl sang songs.

He would carry me down to the couch in the cool cellar when the heat upstairs was too scorching hot to bear, and we would cuddle. His favorite song was "A Bicycle Built for Two."

I would be Daisy Daisy and he would pretend to be my boyfriend.

Let me think a minute here, Margarete told herself. Wait. Something's wrong. What am I forgetting? She sat on the edge of her wooden chair, head bent, her fingers taut on her knees. Hadn't we been singing that song just before he took that awful crashing tumble down the cellar stairs? She could picture him lying there, his neck bent funny, covered with vinegar beets from the crock, the galvanized pail by his head slippery with blood. She remembered running across the field to a neighbor who called her mother in the city. Her fingers trembling, Margarete typed:

Mother squinted at the scene, still wearing her factory apron. She lifted Uncle Earl's dead arm with the point of her shoe, her hands on her hips, her mouth a wrinkled O.

"It will cost us something to bury him," she told me.

Mother took me back to the factory where I sat as still as I was able in the corner until closing time.

Sister Margarete swayed in her chair, her eyes closed, her heart aching. She gathered the wooden rosary beads against her throat. A sudden picture had appeared in her mind of a beautiful woman all glittery screaming down from the top of the cellar stairs. A clear picture.

"Earl, you filthy goat. Put that little girl down."

"Go back to the dead," he screamed, stumbling up the stairs, his eyes crazy.

Sister Margarete remembered hiding behind the couch until long after the fighting stopped, until the front door closed and the house was quiet. When, finally, she peeked out and saw Uncle Earl twisted and bleeding at the bottom of the stairs, she had run to the neighbor.

Now she sat rigid in her chair, overwhelmed by the memory of something that had happened seventy years earlier to the little girl she once had been. All of the people were long dead—her mother, her father, Uncle Earl. Delia.

Outside her window, Sister Margarete watched the handyman, Herb, pushing his wheelbarrow to the vegetable garden—a sweet man, polite, childlike, helpful and yet, as with other men all her life—the smell of him when he came close was intolerable.

In the distance, the bronze bell signaled the hour for Vespers, the evening prayer, her favorite service of the day. As she had for sixty years, she would sing the hymns and recite the ancient psalms in the comfort of the chapel, in the company of the other sisters in the convent.

Perhaps tonight, in the silent time that followed the service, she could begin to drive the smell of pick-me-up from her nostrils.

PSALM 36

An oracle is within my heart,
concerning the sinfulness of the wicked.
There is no fear of God before his eyes.
For in his own eyes he flatters himself
too much to detect or hate his sin.
The words of his mouth are wicked and deceitful.
he has ceased to be wise and to do good.
Even on his bed he plots evil;
he commits himself to a sinful course.
and does not reject what is wrong . . .

φφφ

Betty Hyland writes on mental illness because she had a son who was schizophrenic. She has published in many periodicals. *A Thousand Cloudy Days,* won the Eugene V. Debs essay award for 1993. She has recently expanded it (Infinity Pub) to include previously published essays, newspaper articles, magazine stories, NIMH accounts, op-ed pieces and profiles of the mentally ill. It brings readers into hospitals, board and care homes, private homes, jails and the streets.

CBS developed her young adult story about a schizophrenic boy, *The Girl with the Crazy Brother* (Watts), into an after-school special directed by Diane Keaton and starring Patricia Arquette. In 1989 Betty received a grant from Caltech to study mental health in China.

She has written four cozies set in a monastery, featuring The Benedictine Bloodhounds.

In addition to Sisters in Crime, she runs The Writers of Chantilly, editing their anthologies; is a member of Alliance for the Mentally Ill groups in the Washington, DC area and in California, advising members who want to write their stories; and she is a member of P.E.N. USA West.

SISTERS AND BROTHERS
by Audrey Liebross

Sisters should never marry brothers. I figured that out when my sister's marriage began plunging into an abyss after twenty-six years. By then, of course, it was much too late.

Susan and I had gotten engaged the same day to Chuck and Keith, respectively. We married in a double wedding. We bought houses two doors apart in a typical Maryland suburb. Our kids all grew up together, although, by now, they're on their own, each living out of town.

Things were fine in the beginning, at least for Keith and me. However, it didn't take Susan more than a year to figure out that Keith's older brother turned pretty mean when he'd had a few two many beers. But with Jennifer already on the way, it wasn't as if Susan could really up and leave. And after all, he didn't abuse her physically, though his door slamming and cursing made it awfully hard for her to face the neighbors the next day. So Susan and Chuck stayed together, though every five years or so, they'd hit some kind of crisis or other. Each time, they managed to reconcile, usually with lots of intervention from Keith and me, but it was always touch-and-go. And things seemed to go downhill once their kids left the nest.

Susan's and Chuck's marital difficulties, unsurprisingly, created lots of problems for Keith and me. Over a two-day period, Susan called me in tears twice, once when Chuck had gotten drunk, and once when, enraged over her nagging, he had smashed her antique mirror. I urged her to move in with us for a few nights, but Keith wouldn't hear of it, not wanting to be placed in the awkward position of offering a home to his brother's runaway wife. I tried to convince Keith to talk his brother into entering counseling with Susan, but Keith kept saying their problems were none of our business and that we should stay out of it. I noticed he didn't stay out of it, though—I overheard him advising Chuck how to hide assets.

Susan came over one Saturday in July when Chuck and Keith were out together. She plunked herself down at my kitchen table, and started ruminating about what life would be like without Chuck. Much as I had to admit that splitting up seemed the sensible thing to do, especially after Chuck had refused counseling, I worried about the effect of their breakup on my own marriage. "Are you really thinking about a divorce after all these years?" I asked.

"Not really. I'd probably wind up in lousy

shape financially." Susan turned red and lowered her voice. "Actually, I'm thinking of killing him, instead." I laughed, relieved. I'd blown off steam by threatening to kill my husband a couple of times, myself—most recently, when Keith had encouraged his brother to get a Post Office box, so Susan wouldn't find out if Chuck bought any separate investments.

"No, I mean it," she said, seeing my reaction. I stopped laughing. I just looked at her, not knowing what to think.

Over the next few weeks, I watched Susan carefully. Was it possible that my sister had been serious? She didn't seem to be crazy—she kept going to work, doing her laundry, and getting her hair done, but maybe it doesn't always show when someone has fallen off the deep end. Should I be doing something: talking to a psychiatrist or the police, warning Keith, warning Chuck—anything to make sure that my only sibling wasn't really planning to do away with her husband? Then Susan got involved in another of her string of new hobbies (this time, car repair – better than her last: steer roping), and I breathed a sigh of relief.

Unfortunately, my sister's keeping herself busy with her community college auto workshop didn't stop Chuck from acting like a jerk. The tension climbed between Keith and me each time Susan called with a report of Chuck's latest transgressions. After Keith spent the night on the fold-out bed in the den because of one of our increasingly frequent arguments over his brother's behavior, I suggested he move in with Chuck and let Susan stay with me for awhile. Keith wouldn't hear of it.

Susan, despite my earlier worries, was the calmest of the four of us. She just kept crawling under her car, changing the oil and doing God knows what else. When I asked her how she could stay so serene when both marriages were falling apart, she just smiled at me enigmatically.

Things kept deteriorating. Chuck moved out of his and Susan's bedroom and I threw Keith out of ours. I again suggested a cooling off period with the brothers living in one house and the sisters in the other, but Keith still wouldn't agree. "I'm #@$!! if I'll let your *%$&$! sister chase me out of my *&%#!! house!" he snarled, slamming the door as he stormed off.

Meanwhile, Susan, immersed in her new hobby, performed miracles on our aging Toyota. (She was too late for our Windstar. It had died a few weeks earlier, and Keith and I had nearly come to blows trying unsuccessfully to decide on a replacement). Perhaps trying to get back into her husband's good graces, Susan began a long list of improvements to his SUV. I was sure Chuck was staying in the marriage only long enough to take advantage of her newly acquired automotive skills, but Susan shrugged and said she didn't care – she needed the practice.

Things came to a head one day in January, when both Susan and I had taken vacation days from work. Susan came over, smiling, wiping her hands on a towel, her jeans covered with grease. "I'm ready," she announced.

"Ready to leave Chuck?" I asked, thinking that I, too, might be ready to leave my marriage, but wondering how she could be so sunny at the prospect.

"No, silly, ready to kill him." The light bulb in my head finally went on about Susan's new hobby. She cheerfully confirmed my suspicions. "I've got his car rigged so, after about fifteen miles, he'll lose control. I've planned it to happen after bowling tonight, on Morrow Road." Morrow Road was a curvy, twisting highway with a cliff on one side. "If anyone figures out later that I've tampered with it, I'll just say I must have repaired it wrong."

I couldn't believe the choice that Susan was leaving me: betray my sister or let her husband—the brother of my own spouse—drive off a cliff. I shooed her out of the house with the excuse that I needed to take a shower, but I really just wanted to think.

I agonized for awhile, shampooed my hair, and agonized some more. Finally, I decided that I had to act. I dialed Keith's number at work. First, I worried that he wouldn't be in, then I worried that he would. As he picked up the phone, I finally made up my mind what to say. "I have a big favor to ask," I began. "I know you don't like the guys in Keith's Friday night bowling group, but Susan is worried about him." Taking a deep breath, I continued, "Could you go with him tonight?" Keith agreed. They drove off later that evening in Chuck's newly "repaired" SUV, and never bothered either of us again.

As I said, sisters should never marry brothers. If Susan and I hadn't, maybe neither of us would be a widow. But then, if I weren't a widow, I wouldn't have a hefty life insurance payout invested in blue chip stocks. My newfound independence sure makes up for the occasional twinges of regret.

φφφ

Audrey Liebross is married and has three sons ranging in age from twelve to thirty-one. When she's not writing mysteries or being a mom, she can be found at her desk in the legal office of a federal agency. She wants all her friends and family to know that this story is not in any way autobiographical, and that she is grateful to have her husband and sister, instead of the ones in the story.

THE BUTLER DIDN'T DO IT
by Maria Lima

The telegram said it all.

AUNT DEAD STOP BUTLER DID
IT STOP FLY SOONEST STOP
—GERALD

It took a few minutes for it to sink in. My aunt Clara was dead, and evidently her butler was the culprit.

Of course, news of her death didn't exactly come as a surprise. Not that she was old, by any means, but at sixty-eight, Clara hadn't changed much from her wild childhood. The sixties had been *very* good to her. I'd expected to hear that she'd died in some sort of mountain-climbing accident, or jumping out of a plane, not to get some ten-word message that said everything and explained nothing.

I tried to call my cousin but got his voice mail. As usual, he was avoiding the situation. Really, who uses telegrams anymore? Not answering the phone meant he wouldn't have to talk to me, and that meant there'd be no ride waiting when I arrived at the airport. I hoped my credit card would stretch to cover a trans-Atlantic trip.

My fulltime "real world" job and nearly fulltime writing schedule left little time or money for expensive vacations in the English countryside. I write mystery novels starring werewolves, vampires, and ghouls in contemporary America. Although I hadn't been to Clara's in nearly three years, I'd sent her both of my published books, and several of my short stories. She'd always been extremely supportive, sure that one day I'd break out and become wildly popular. From her mouth to the book-buying public's ears.

I rented a car in London, choosing possible death by bad driving over my other choices—an interminable trip by bus, an equally unbearable local train, or an astronomically expensive limousine. Gerald could have at least sent the estate Rolls for me. Oh, yeah, well maybe not. Jamison, the erstwhile butler, was also the chauffeur. I guess that was out of the question if he were really being considered as a suspect.

Chalfont is an Edwardian monstrosity that could have used a heck of a lot more maintenance from my oblivious aunt. On several hundred acres of meadows and forest, the estate had been the happy hunting lodge for several generations of idle-rich sons until the last one had lost the entire estate to Clara's great-uncle Albert in an unfettered night of gambling, whoring, and drinking. Albert died utterly unrepentant, having celebrated his ill-gotten gains every day of his miserably long life. Because he'd had no children, Clara inherited the whole package, including, surprisingly enough, a decent income with which to maintain the estate and to allow her to live the life of the cheerily and unapologetically unemployed. She'd also inherited Jamison, a paragon of butlers and the fourth generation of Jamison men to serve at Chalfont.

I parked in the back courtyard and went in through the kitchen door, opening it onto the scene of Mrs. Cooper, the cook, and Dina, the housemaid, sitting at the staff dining table.

They both looked up, startled. If I hadn't known better, I'd have thought they'd both been enjoying a joke.

"Miss Lindsay," exclaimed the cook. "Let me get you some tea." She helped me pull my heavy bag over the threshold.

"T'aint much," she continued, "but I baked this morning." She pulled out a platter with scones and tea biscuits and poured me a cup of steaming tea.

"Thank you," I said, warming my hands around the cup. I was still a little shaky from the drive and didn't really want to go into the main part of the house. It was a dismal monstrosity that belonged in a suspense movie and not in real life. All the rooms were damp and dark with the gloom of antique windows and heavy draperies. I'd always felt uncomfortable there, even though I adored Aunt Clara.

"Mrs. C, can you tell me what happened?" Knowing Gerald's taste for melodrama, I didn't for a minute believe that Jamison had anything to do with her death.

"Exsanguination," proclaimed Dina in a funereal tone. She was a small, quiet girl, not normally given to strange pronouncements.

"What?" I exclaimed, not sure I'd heard her right.

"Now, Dina," said Mrs. Cooper, frowning and shooting Dina a sharp glance, "don't be telling tales out of school. You know Doctor Waldron said it were probably summat else what caused it."

"What do you mean?" I was puzzled.

The cook and Dina looked at each other fixedly, as if each were daring the other to speak. Mrs. Cooper was the first to talk.

"He found her in her bed, Miss. She were right pale," explained the cook. "But the doctor thought it were natural. Like a blood disease or summat. She were kind enough to come out directly, even though she were at church and all."

"Doctor been out here lots these days, with your aunt feeling sickly," said Dina, "but Mr. Gerald insisted on ringing up the Constable, Miss. He blamed Jamison. Constable Macdonald come and took Jamison with him. Said they'd keep 'im awhile, to help him in his inquiries." She nodded her head, as if remembering something. "Mr. Gerald said that'd be just fine. That'd be long enough."

I was getting a little confused. My aunt had been sick, had apparently died of a disease, but my cousin had blamed the butler? I knew Gerald had always disliked Jamison, but mostly because the butler had never allowed him to pull the whiny brat routine, not even when Gerald was a boy.

"Where is my cousin now?" I asked. I planned on having a long, if distasteful, talk with him.

"He left an hour ago," said Dina. She looked at me with a smirk. "He took the Rolls."

That figured. My aunt was dead less than forty-eight hours and Gerald had already appropriated her Rolls Royce. Well, he'd soon have another think coming. I knew what was in Clara's will, since she'd e-mailed me a copy earlier in the year. I chuckled at the thought of what Gerald would say when he realized that Clara had left everything to the servants.

I sat bolt upright, spilling my tea. My aunt had left the bulk of the estate in a trust for Jamison and the rest of the staff. I wasn't sure of the amount of money, but I knew it wasn't small potatoes. A house the size of Chalfont required a fortune for upkeep and taxes, and Clara had never pinched pennies. The money had been well invested and had grown quite handsomely over the years. Could someone as loyal, kind and trustworthy as Jamison really *have* killed my aunt for her money?

"I think it'd be best if you went upstairs and took a rest, Miss," said Mrs. Cooper, wiping up my mess. "Dina, let's get Miss Lindsay settled."

Dina jumped up from her chair, eager to help. "Yes, Ma'am," she said, and grabbed the handle of my suitcase. "I've cleaned up one of the guest rooms for her."

"I'll tell Mr. Gerald you're resting when he returns, Miss Lindsay," said Mrs. Cooper. "That way you'll not be disturbed."

"Thank you, Dina," I said. If I could get my computer hooked up, I could access a copy of the will on my laptop.

"Where is my cousin staying?" I asked Dina, as we entered the hallway next to the bedrooms.

"In the master suite," she replied, snickering. "We told him it weren't fit, but he made me." I chuckled. That suite of rooms hadn't been lived in since Great-Uncle Albert's days. Clara had preferred a smaller suite on the other side of the house. I hoped Gerald liked sleeping with spiders.

My cousin's actions were too transparent—commandeering the Rolls, setting himself up in the master suite—as if he thought that would establish him as the master of Chalfont. He was in for a surprise.

I quickly found the file I was looking for. I was right. All of Clara's assets, less a few token personal bequests, were to be held in a trust administered by her solicitor and benefiting all the persons living in the house at the time that she was declared dead.

According to the specifics of the will, no one person would benefit from any of the money. The staff was to continue at Chalfont and care for the house and grounds, as if Clara were still there. Each would get a small bequest plus continue their current salary, with appropriate annual increases in pay. As trustee, Jamison would be in charge of household expenses, including pay raises and spending for the upkeep of the house and grounds. In fact, he'd basically be doing the same job he was doing now, and the job would be his until he died. On his death, the job of trustee would be turned over to his nearest relative or designee, with the same caveats, and so on.

I couldn't see any motive for killing my aunt. The staff had a good deal whether or not Clara was dead or alive, unless Jamison had figured out some way to bleed the trust dry. But that was unlikely. To what end? He'd always struck me as a career butler. To my layman's eye, the provisions of the trust looked pretty straightforward. There was even a clause that made the whole thing invalid if Clara's death was found to have been caused by any or all of the persons named as benefiting from the will.

I sat staring at my screen wondering what I wasn't seeing here. Why would Gerald think that Jamison had killed my aunt? What motive would he have had?

"What're you doing?" my cousin's voice startled me out of my thoughts. I quickly glanced up at the screen, relieved to find that my screensaver had kicked in.

I closed the laptop and turned towards him. "So, where were you?" I asked. "Taking a joy ride in Auntie's Rolls?" My voice was sarcastic.

He frowned at me, getting that silly pompous look. It meant that he thought he was being responsible. "I was making arrangements," he said, puffing up his chest.

"Fine," I said, crossing my arms. "So what are they?"

"What are what?" he asked.

"The arrangements. What are they?" I looked at him. He hadn't been taking care of himself. I'm not one to talk, working full time and writing until all hours doesn't exactly make me a candidate for a Wheaties box, but Gerald looked as if he'd been up all night. Maybe he had.

"The funeral will be tomorrow," he said. "Montmorency and Sons will take care of things.

"We'll have the viewing tonight." He looked down and mumbled something I didn't quite catch. It almost sounded as if he'd said "if she cooperates".

I frowned. "What did you say, Gerald?"

"Nothing," he said quickly. "Would you like to pay your respects?"

Oh, God, it suddenly hit me. "She's here?" I asked. I had assumed my aunt's body had been taken to the funeral home. I should have remembered my cousin's obsession with the whole "lord of the manor" thing.

"Of course she is," he said. "She's in the chapel. It wouldn't do to have the neighboring gentry go to a mortuary."

I could picture it now. Gerald would be dressed in his best shiny black suit, holding court in the drawing room while visitors traipsed out to the chapel to do whatever it is one does when one comes to view the recently deceased.

"Do you want to go pay your respects?" he repeated.

"Yes," I stated. "I think I will go see her." I wasn't too happy with the idea, but figured I should do something as a family member.

"Would you like me to escort you?" he asked, holding out his hand. He may have been trying to be kind, but I could see his hand shaking a little. It was probably damp, too.

"No, thanks, I'll go on my own. It's only Aunt Clara." I sounded a lot more sure of myself than I was. It was a little weird having the dead body of your possibly murdered aunt in the same house, but the chapel was off one wing and not really in the main section. It's not as if it was next door to my bedroom or anything. And after all, she *was* dead.

I wiped my hands on my jeans. This wing was darker and much colder, too, as if neither light nor heat could reach this far. The hallway boasted beautiful stained glass panels that, gorgeous as they were, let in precious little ambient light. Clara had never shown much interest in the chapel and the lighting hadn't been updated. A few flickering bulbs threw off a pale yellow light that made the passageway seem even darker by comparison.

I was hoping the main overhead lights in the chapel still worked, or I was hightailing it out of there. I fully admit to being a bit of a chicken. Maybe it's the novels I write but I have way too active of an imagination.

I reached the door and pushed it open slowly. A soft flickering light came from inside, up by the altar in front. My mouth was dry and I was breathing too fast. Clara's body was laid out on a bier, surrounded by candles, dozens of them in tall holders, like something out of a "B"-movie. What had Gerald been thinking? I halfway expected to hear Count Dracula's seductive "Gut Eve-ning" as I walked in.

The candles made it worse than having no light at all. I suppose shuttering the chapel windows had been done out of respect, but I didn't like it.

I made my way around the outside edge of the chapel and towards the back, where the main switchbox was, staying as far as possible from Clara. I knew I was being silly, but I just couldn't go any closer. Not in this dark. From here, she looked as if she were sleeping. It didn't look like her really, especially not in that high-neck, demure white nightgown. She'd been more likely to sleep in lurid purple sweats or in the nude.

I reached the back wall and found the array of light switches. Pressing one after the other, I realized that either a fuse had blown or that the electricity had been shut off to the chapel. That was enough. There was no way I'd stay here in this Hammer-film set.

"May I help you?"

I shrieked and jumped back against the wall.

"Jamison?" My voice shook, the word emerging in a small squeal.

"Yes, miss," he replied, his voice as calm and soothing as ever. I'd always admired his beautiful voice. Always peaceful and quiet, he'd easily handled my volatile aunt.

"I thought..." I began, fumbling for words. How on earth was I going to say this?

"Thought that I'd been incarcerated, Miss Lindsay?" He seemed to be amused.

"Yes."

"Constable Macdonald finished with his inquiries, Miss. So I came back." He turned and gestured for me to walk ahead of him, effectively turning me toward the door. "I'm sure you wish to return to the main house. I'll send for someone to see to the electricity. I'm sure there's only a minor problem." He deftly turned me in the direction of the door.

"Yes, thank you, Jamison." I mumbled, and hurried out of the chapel. Funny, I really *was* sure he hadn't killed Aunt Clara, but his being there in the dark chapel had really unnerved me. I'd almost gotten the feeling that he hadn't wanted me to approach my aunt too closely. Not that I'd particularly wanted to, but still…

φ

I settled in for a short nap and by the time I woke up, it was already getting close to dark. The first of the neighbors would probably start arriving soon, in time for a quick pop into the chapel and then out for cocktails and hors d'oeuvres. It wouldn't do to arrive too early and miss the refreshments.

I wanted to go back to the chapel before anyone else got there. Not only did I want to make sure that the electricity was working, but I really thought I should at least make some semblance of prayer or something. I wasn't much for religion or anything, but my aunt had been a fun and unusual relative, often the source of much of the material in my novels. No one could make up some of the stuff she'd done. She deserved more than a perfunctory visit.

My heart sank when I saw that Gerald was in the hallway outside the chapel. So much for a little privacy. He was standing still, staring at the closed doors.

"Going in, cuz?" I asked, a little sarcastically.

He whirled, eyes wide and mouth opening & shutting like a fish gasping for air. I'd never noticed how much Gerald reminded me of a guppy until now.

"Wha—?" he gasped, stumbling a little as he stepped away from me.

I grinned, enjoying this. "What's wrong, Gerald? Scared to go in?" I wasn't above mocking him for the same fears I had. At least I'd actually gone in before. Okay, so I hadn't actually stayed very long.

He grimaced and tried to compose himself, straightening his jacket and smoothing what was left of his hair.

"I was just taking a moment of silence before entering," he said, his voice icy and almost mean. "Aunt Clara deserves our utmost respect."

"Yeah, whatever," I said, and moved to step around him so I could reach the door handle. "Did Jamison get the lights working yet?"

"Jamison?" His voice became a mousy squeak.

I was getting impatient. He was blocking my way and I wanted to go in and make sure everything was ready for the viewing. Funny, now that Gerald was here, my earlier nervousness was gone and all I wanted to do was to get this over with.

"Yes, Jamison," I said, pushing him out of the way and opened the door. "He told me he'd get someone to check on the electricity. It wasn't working when I was here a little while ago."

"Jamison can't be here," he said, gulping hard, his voice still shaky.

I stopped and turned to face him, briefly noting that the electric wall sconces were glowing with a soft light. Good.

"Gerald, what is your problem? Jamison was released after talking to the police. He's back on duty here. Evidently, he's no longer a suspect." I stared at Gerald's face, which seemed to be much paler than normal. Hard to tell, since his normal complexion is that of a mushroom.

"He..." My cousin couldn't seem to get the words out.

"He what?"

Gerald stammered again and then stopped to take a breath. As he opened his mouth to speak, I saw him glance over my shoulder. His face froze and instead of words, he let out a long wail and pointed behind me.

I spun around, my brain slowly processing the words my cousin was shrieking, as I took in the sight in front of me.

"She's gone, she's gone, she's gone." Gerald's voice got higher with each word.

Although the sconces were on, the area around the altar remained dark. The candles were still the only source of light up there, illuminated nothing more than the empty bier. My aunt's body had vanished.

I swallowed hard and started to move when Gerald grabbed me.

"No!" he said, hoarsely. "Don't."

I pulled my arm and forced it out of his grasp. I needed to get closer to see. My brain raced. I knew we needed to call the Constable, Jamison, anybody. I didn't want to be alone here. Gerald, in his current state, didn't count.

Maybe the funeral home had mistakenly come early. I walked up the aisle, my steps slow, barely aware of Gerald behind me. Moving closer, I halfway expected to see a business card from Montmorency & Sons on the bier. Like when a realtor leaves a card behind to let you know she's shown your house while you were out. My mind was practically babbling.

Of course, there was nothing there but a satin pillow. In fact, it still had the impression of Clara's head on it and one lone gray hair. As I started to head for the main switch panel to turn on the rest of the lights, I realized what Gerald was saying.

"She's going to come back. She knows it was me." He blubbered around the words, crying and covering his face with his hands.

"Gerald?" I said, not wanting to understand what I was hearing. Was he trying to tell me that Aunt Clara *had* been murdered? And that *he'd* done it?

He looked up, his face tear-stained. "She's coming back for me."

"Coming back?" I realized what he was saying. "Gerald, get a grip. Aunt Clara is dead."

He nodded, still blubbering. "I saw them. They didn't know."

He glanced towards the empty bier. "And now she's walking the night. The other night, I came to ask her for some money. My business..." He looked at me with an apologetic glance.

"But I couldn't find her," he continued. "So I went up to see the butler. To see if he knew where she was. His door was open. They were there together. It was horrible."

I was appalled, bemused, and more than a little confused. So my aunt had been having an affair with her butler. It wasn't exactly "the thing" in the local circles, but Clara had always marched to her own beat.

"Blood," whispered Gerald.

He finally looked at me, his eyes shiny and round. "He was drinking her blood, and then, she did the same to him. So, I had to do it."

I stared at him, not believing what I heard. Was my aunt into some sort of Goth weirdness? At her age? She'd always been a little strange, but this was too much to believe.

"I had it all worked out," he continued, his voice stronger now, as he gained confidence in his actions.

"I'd report her dead. Then blame Jamison. I was coming to the chapel to make sure it was permanent with her, too. But it's too late. She's already risen." He started to walk towards the bier, his movements jerky and unnatural. "Now she'll come for me. With him." He turned back to face me. "It's like your books, but it's real."

"Gerald," I started walking toward him. My only thought was to get him to a doctor, and soon. He'd really flipped. A low keening sound came out of his throat as he stared past me toward the chapel door we'd just come in.

My legs gave out when I heard a low, yet, cheerful voice behind me, and I fell into the front pew with a thud.

"Darling, child, it's all true, you know."

I didn't want to look at the source of those words. I knew it was Clara's voice. Clara — the same person that had been lying dead on that bier just a few hours ago.

She continued speaking, a definite hint of amusement in her tone, "I'm afraid Gerald discovered our little secret."

"You see," said Clara, sitting down in the pew behind me. "I found out a few months ago that I had a fatal blood disorder. That's when Jamison did what he's always done. Take care of me and of Chalfont. After all, I didn't want to die. I wanted to stay at Chalfont and enjoy my life. Besides, who would take care of Mrs. Cooper, and young Dina?"

I turned, half afraid to look directly at her. Gerald was making incoherent moaning sounds behind me. This could *not* be happening. Part of me wanted to believe her, the other part wondered if I'd fallen into some bizarre nightmarish plot from one of my own novels. I avoided the cliché of pinching myself—I definitely knew I was awake.

Still dressed in the incongruous white nightie, my aunt looked healthier than she had any right to be, a self-satisfied smile on her face. She grinned and showed off some rather pointed incisors, and then reached over and patted my hand. Her skin felt cool, as if she'd been out in the night air. Come to think of it, she probably had.

I pulled back my hand. I wasn't sure about any of this.

"Clara," I said, finding that I could still speak. "You can't mean what I think do."

Clara laughed; a delighted sound that bounced around the echoing chapel walls. She motioned for Jamison to come closer. He'd been standing in the shadows behind her.

"Yes, dearest, it is true, although hard to believe. Jamison only told me when he realized I was dying. He gallantly offered and I accepted." She turned to him and smiled.

Jamison bowed slightly and said in his best butler's voice, "Anything for Miss Clara."

My aunt reached over and patted my hand again, continuing her story. "So I rewrote my will. I figured I'd falsify my death at some point and then come back as a distant cousin or something when it was necessary to keep up appearances."

She looked at her undead butler and smiled. "I set up the trust with Jamison's great-great-grandson. He's my solicitor as it turns out. Young Jamey will administer the trust and Jamison will run the house. When it's necessary, he'll "retire", and then his "cousin" will come into service here. It's perfect! You do realize that he's been here for a very long time?" She looked concerned, as if she wanted to be sure I fully understood.

I managed a sickly smile. I'd always heard of the four generations of Jamison men. Could she be implying that it was *this* Jamison all along?

Her smile grew wider into a Cheshire Cat grin as she saw the comprehension in my eyes. Now I could really see the sharp points of her new teeth gleaming. I was beginning to believe her. She'd never looked like that before. She was positively glowing.

"But why the bier," I stammered, finally accepting that Clara was serious. "Why the whole death thing? Couldn't you have just kept on for a while?"

At this, Gerald broke into loud sobs and fell into a crumpling heap on the floor.

Clara frowned at the sight of my cousin weeping like a toddler. "It was Gerald's fault," she replied. "We weren't going to set up my death for at least twenty more years, but your cousin forced the issue. He wasn't supposed to have been here last weekend. After he saw us, he reported my "death" to the authorities, making me play out this silly charade." She tugged on the neck of the nightgown and frowned.

Clara's voice grew hard as she turned her gaze on Gerald. "Is that why you told them, Gerald? And had Jamison arrested? To *punish* me? What were you planning to do?"

Gerald moaned again. "I'd seen part of your will when I came up that weekend. I went upstairs to confront you."

His voice became as whiny as a child's as he continued. "I was your nephew and needed the money more than those servants of yours.

"And when I saw the two of you, I knew I had to do something. I figured that the police would keep him until daylight and then it would be all over for him. After that, I could come back and move you out into the sun. Then you'd really be dead. And you wouldn't be an abomination and I'd get the money since he'd be gone, too."

His voice was still shaking but he stood up and thrust out his chest. "I had it all figured out. I sent a telegram to Lindsay, and then called the constable."

I groaned, realizing that that was what Mrs. Cooper and Dina had meant about the doctor. I'd gotten the telegram early Saturday afternoon. When I'd arrived, today, Monday morning, they'd implied that Clara had "died" just yesterday. Gerald had found her "dead" on Sunday and reported it then. As usual, Gerald had messed up and done it in the wrong order. Eventually, he would have been found out. I was pretty sure that both Mrs. C and Dina were aware of this whole set-up.

"So, what now?" I asked with more than a little bravado. I wasn't too sure I wanted to hear the answer. If this were one of my novels, or a TV show, the "bad guys" would be getting rid of the witnesses. That would be Gerald...and me.

Clara laughed again, obviously enjoying herself. "Dearest Lindsay, you don't really think I would let anything happen to you?" She folded her hand around mine, giving it a small squeeze. This time, I didn't draw it back.

"Besides, I'm sure that you wouldn't mind a few anecdotes from the real world?" She winked at me broadly.

I began to see the possibilities. I could always use more grist for my writing mill. It wasn't easy to come up with fresh angles for my books. Modern audiences were rather jaded these days. I suppose it was overexposure, but new books were getting harder to write. I'd even resorted to borrowing heavily from classic Greek and Roman tales. An infusion of new blood, so to speak, might be just what I needed. After all, who would ever believe it was real?

Clara stood up abruptly and motioned with her hand. In one swift movement, Jamison was past me and had grabbed Gerald by the arm. He'd been trying to sneak out the back.

He stood there cowering under Clara's gaze, as Jamison held him immobile. Clara smiled and delicately licked her lips. "I think we can work something out." She looked at Jamison and laughed, "For the both of you."

φ

That was three years ago. For some bizarre reason (maybe it was the latest crop of vampire TV shows?) my books were selling like the latest fancy coffee drink at Starbucks. Not that I was complaining. I'd been able to quit my day job and write fulltime now.

I still kept in touch with everyone via e-mail, especially Mrs. Cooper and Dina, who'd bought new computers once my aunt's will was probated. Clara had been duly "buried" and mourned and her butler had taken over the running of the house.

As for Gerald, Mrs. C reported that everyone in town agreed how very lucky he'd been to be able to obtain a position at Chalfont after his business failed. How kind of Mr. Jamison to think of his late employer's relation and to offer him the job of valet. And Mr. Gerald with no training, either.

The latest rumor was that a distant cousin of Aunt Clara's had written to Mr. Jamison. It seems her people had immigrated to New Zealand some time ago, and she'd recently found out about her relatives in England. In fact, she might be coming for a visit soon.

φφφ

Born in Matanzas, Cuba, **Maria Lima** emigrated to the U.S. at age three, and has been writing and editing every since she learned to pick up a pencil. An avid mystery, science fiction and fantasy fan, she's written on subjects as varied as marketing for the Web to author interviews and book reviews. Her paranormal mystery novel, *Matters of the Blood* (Juno Books, March 2007) merges the world of the supernatural with romance and murder in the Texas Hill Country. Maria is beyond pleased with her Agatha nomination for "The Butler Didn't Do It". She is also co-editor of "Chesapeake Crimes II". Visit her at her Web site: www.thelima.com.

DEADLY DETOUR
by Debbi Mack

Late July is no time to be sitting in a car, in a parking lot, in Ocean City, Maryland. It was stinking hot, and moist air pressed in through the open windows and enveloped me like a blanket. I glanced at my watch and cursed Mendez for her lateness.

I'm too old for this, I thought. Women pushing forty should be working in offices, not in the field. Sure, work in an office. Answer phones, attend meetings, push paper—sounded like slow death by boredom. Of course, how exciting was waiting for someone outside a seedy hotel, an unringing cell phone in my lap. Intelligence work is so glamorous, providing the chance to visit so many exotic locales, such as this one. Such as the many I had visited during my 15-year stint with the agency.

"Doomed," I said, aloud, to no one. I wasn't sure if I was talking about myself or the Bayside Villas.

A set of low, rectangular white stucco boxes, the Bayside Villas looked strangely like white frosted cakes in the moonlight, their windows trimmed in "food coloring" blue. The sound of a yapping dog and a TV set blaring somewhere did little to lift the status of the place.

"What a dump!" I said, imitating Elizabeth Taylor's imitation of Bette Davis in the movie *Who's Afraid of Virginia Woolf.*

I stared at the door to Unit 8, as if that would make Mendez appear sooner. So far, it wasn't working. In the window to Unit 7, the curtain moved for the second time. I smiled.

"Nervous?" I said. Probably afraid I was casing the joint. As if any sane burglar would waste his time here.

A jazz piano tune floated from the dashboard radio. I closed my eyes, opened them a second later. Not good to keep your eyes closed too long at this job. The distant neon circles of a double-decker Ferris wheel bobbed with numbing regularity over the flat rooftops. The bay waters swooshed at intervals against a nearby bulkhead.

Another twenty minutes ticked by. A breeze fragile as a kitten's breath eased through the car, carrying with it the scent of creosote-treated wood. Sweat tickled my neck. Wearily, I wiped it away. The Ferris wheel went through countless cycles.

The Unit 7 curtain moved again, was held longer this time, then dropped.

So what was that all about? Surreptitious interest? Paranoia? Maybe my paranoia. Maybe it had nothing to do with me. Still, it wouldn't hurt to leave for a while. Nothing was up here. And, unless she was in some sort of huge trouble, Mendez should eventually return the message I'd left on her cell phone, let me know she got in okay.

As I turned the ignition key, the door to Unit 7 flew open. A young woman shot out and ran toward my car. Her face was pale, her hair long and dark. She wore a baggy dress, several sizes too large, out of which her skinny arms and legs stuck ridiculously. A large plastic purse on her arm slapped her side as she ran.

I realized that the immense dress was accommodating an immensely-pregnant belly. She moved with amazing speed for one so far along in her maternity. She ran up to my window and leaned in, gasping. She was just a kid, complete with button nose and freckles.

"Help," she screamed.

A tall and thin, but muscular, man in a tank top and olive green pants appeared in the open doorway. The light from the room revealed something tucked in his waistband—a gun.

"Get in," I said. As she ran to the passenger's side, I leaned over to unlock the door. Meanwhile, the man had bolted from the room and was racing toward my car. He had the gun in his hand now.

"Hurry," I yelled. She opened the door and flung herself inside. I took off, tires squealing. I made a mental note of the man's white-blonde hair, dark complexion, and the deep scar on his left cheek, in case I ever had to pick him out of a line-up. A line-up was the kind of place I would have expected to see such a face. He did me the kindness of not shooting holes in my car we sped off.

I made an arbitrary right into the great traffic riptide of Ocean Highway in mid-season.

"Where to?" I said, keeping my eyes on the road and looking out for the occasional idiot tourist that might choose to do a jack rabbit run across my path.

"Make a U-turn. Now."

She spoke with incongruous authority. I glanced at her long enough to see that she had a gun trained on me.

"Firearms," I said, affecting an air of unconcern. "Must we?" I was a bit surprised. Not because she was a kid with a gun. In my line of work, I've seen kids younger than her running around with guns that would make an NRA member weep with envy. And I've been on the wrong end of a gun barrel before. It's just that she really didn't look like that kind of kid. There was nothing street-wise about the face, the attitude, or the way her gun hand shook.

"I said do it!" Her voice spiked into a nervous falsetto on the word "do."

"Why don't you put that away?"

"Why should I?"

"Well, at the risk of offending you, you're not exactly convincing me that you'll actually shoot."

She just stared at me. We were heading into the heart of old-town Ocean City. Traffic had slowed to a crawl, because the Route 50 drawbridge was up. In the distance, I could hear the clatter of the roller coaster and the screams of people on it. The streets were crammed with hordes of college students, young couples, and bikers.

"You're really going to shoot me?" I said. "Right here, in the middle of traffic?"

Reluctantly, she lowered the gun into her lap.

"Better," I said. A cross-street was coming up, so I slowly nosed my way to the left on the one-way road. I managed to get all the way over before the intersection, so I made the turn, went one block over, and turned left again to go back the way I'd come.

She seemed to relax a little, although she didn't let go of the gun. She had that peculiar combination of worldliness and innocence that you see in a kid that's grown up too fast.

"I take it there's somewhere you'd like to go?" I said.

She looked at me sideways. "I wasn't sure if you'd take me there."

"You could always ask."

"Delaware?"

Delaware wasn't far; it wasn't around the corner, either. Ocean City, Maryland is on a thin finger of real estate sandwiched between the Atlantic Ocean and the Isle of Wight Bay. From the southern-most end of town, where we were, it might take twenty minutes to reach the Delaware line, if traffic was good.

"Where in Delaware?" I asked. She could have been talking about a beach town; she could be talking about Wilmington, on the other side of the state.

"Between Fenwick and Bethany Beach? It's not far." She was starting to sound hopeful.

"Well . . ." I wondered where Mendez might be. She might have arrived while all this was going on. The last time I'd tried to reach her, there was no answer. The silence was filled briefly with a bizarre duet courtesy of Miles Davis and a city bus.

The girl reached for her purse and put the gun in it, pulling out a pack of cigarettes and a pink Zippo lighter. She eyed me with curiosity as she lit up, still waiting for an answer.

"Bad for the baby, isn't it?" I said.

"So what are you now, my mother?" Suddenly, she sounded as if she were speaking through clenched vocal chords. She took an aggressive drag on the cigarette, then tapped it extraneously on the sill. "I don't need a lecture on my health, okay?"

"What is this, maybe your eighth month? Ninth?"

She sighed. "Can we skip the maternal chit-chat, mom?"

"And can we skip the sarcasm? I mean, who's doing whom a favor here? Understand this—I'm not your mom. I'm only asking because you look like you could drop that load any second. And I don't make deliveries. So, you start going into labor, I don't care where you say you want to go—we're heading for the nearest hospital. Clear?"

"Okay, whatever." She plucked at her dress, as if to remove lint, and did another tap or two with her cigarette. I supposed this was her notion of acting cool and collected. She looked about as cool as a dental patient waiting for a root canal.

"Don't be a hard ass, okay?" she said. "Anyway, don't worry about all that. Everything will be just fine." Her voice trailed off, as if she didn't quite believe that last point.

As we cruised past the steadily-climbing, numbered side streets, I wondered just what the hell I was doing. My line of work does not encourage voluntary heroics. There's no percentage in it. But when I looked at the waif-like girl, something made me want to help her. Maybe in certain respects, she reminded me of myself. If I thought real hard, I might remember what it was like to be that age and to think you know everything.

The cell phone in my lap chose that moment to ring.

I snatched it up. "Where are you?" I said.

"Stuck on a focking runway." When Mendez was mad, her accent was usually strong. Tonight, it was positively robust, even over the phone's static. "Someone stole my focking cell phone. I had to borrow this nice gentleman's."

"I see."

"We've been here for focking hours. I can't smoke...can't...take a goddamn leak." Her voice began to break up.

"I see." Mendez looks like Rita Morena in her heyday, but swears like a sailor. I wondered what the nice gentleman might be thinking as he overheard this particular conversation.

"Hello? I can't...goddamn thing. I'll... reach...can't..." The phone took a turn for the worse and her words became incomprehensible sound blurbs.

"Hello? Hello?" I said.

"Are you there?" With a blast of static, communication returned. "Jesus, I need a focking cigarette—ay!"

"Call me when you land," I said.

"I can't focking hear you. Our…friend will meet us in the morning. That place…you know."

"Call me!" I yelled, but she was talking at the same time, in semi-decipherable Spanish. Suddenly, we were disconnected. I sighed and dropped the phone in my lap.

The girl eyed me suspiciously. "Who was that?"

"Just an old college pal," I said. I didn't even see her reach for the phone. Next thing I knew, it was in her hand.

"Hey!" I said.

Then she launched it out the window.

"What the hell?" I said. "Lucky for you that's a company phone, or I'd…"

"You'd what?"

I shook my head, as if it would make everything clearer. "What the hell did you do that for?"

"In case."

"In case of what?"

"Forget it. Just drive."

"Hey…hey!" I pointed my finger at her. "I'm inclined to kick your ass out of this car right now."

There was a moment of silence. "I'm sorry." Her voice was subdued.

"Sorry! That's great. I'll probably get docked for the cost of a new phone. Ohh…" At the nearest intersection, I swerved over two lanes, drawing honks from a few critics, and turned onto the side street. I parked the car and pulled a few bucks from my fanny pack.

"Get out. Here's some money. Take the bus. Or not. I don't care. Just take a hike."

I handed over the bills. As she took them, I could see her hand shaking.

"Oh, what is this..." I started to say something, but she had begun crying now and I didn't think she was acting. Soundlessly, at first, tears streamed down her cheeks. Then, with a great inhale of breath, she began sobbing, her shoulders shaking and her arms clutched around her belly.

"I freaked out," she said, in a high, quavering voice. "I'm sorry. I'm really sorry. Please don't leave me here. I'm sorry. Damn it." She wiped the tears away fiercely with the back of her hand.

"What is it with you?" I tried to hide my irritation, with little success.

"I thought maybe you'd call the cops. I thought... I don't know. I don't know what I thought. I just freaked, that's all."

"Okay, okay. We've established that. Christ." I leaned against the seat and waited for the storm to pass. But the tears kept coming.

"Someone was supposed to pick me up...back there," she said, between sobs. "But he never showed. And all I could think... I just had to get out. That man back there. He would have killed me."

I thought of the blond with the scar. "Yeah, he didn't look all that pleasant."

"I didn't know what to do." With her fingers, she raked her hair out of her face, now mottled from crying. "I figured I'd head for our usual place. I figured, maybe my friend got held up or something. Maybe he's there."

"Okay," I said. "Okay, fine."

Mendez was held up on a runway, swearing at her smokeless lot in life. She'd said something about meeting our contact tomorrow morning. What was I going to do until then? Go back to an empty motel room and watch HBO until I fell asleep, probably. The girl was making futile attempts to stem the flow of liquid snot from her nose. Hell, I was halfway to the state line already.

"All right. I'll take you to Delaware. But no more funny stuff, right? I mean it. No guns, no throwing things."

She nodded. "Everything's all fucked up. I don't know what's going on. I hope he's there."

"Right." I hoped like hell he was there, too.

Up Ocean Highway we went, past the towering condos at the north end of town, across the state line, and into Fenwick Island, Delaware. After Fenwick, development became sparse, then dwindled to nothing as we drove past the state park. At sixty miles an hour, the wet ocean breeze blasted through the car, taking the edge off the heat. Sand dunes undulated to our right, providing occasional glimpses of a golden full moon against a velvety black sky.

She had turned pensive now, and it had been a quiet ride. I tried to coax some information, like a name or a home town or something, out of her. But she wasn't talking. I had no idea what I would do if the friend wasn't there. I figured we could cross that bridge when we got to it.

Eventually, she had me turn onto a road leading through a section of tall cattails toward the beach. We crawled up to the foot of a terraced, wooden house on stilts, gray with age and exposure to the elements. Waves pounded on the surf in a soothing, if incessant, roar.

She looked around. "I don't see his car."

"Maybe he's not here yet," I said. Or maybe he's not coming, I thought. My heart sank.

We got out of the car. I followed her up a flight of steep, rickety steps to a small landing in front of a weather-beaten green door. It was unlocked and we strolled right in.

"Travis!" she called. The room, dimly lit with a bare-bulb ceiling light, featured an old sofa that looked like it was upholstered in burlap and a table with three plain wooden chairs. No one answered. A short, dark hallway led to another room.

"Damn." She began pacing, chewing on her thumbnail.

I sighed and crossed the room to the shadeless window. "What now?"

She didn't answer. I glanced outside. From our vantage point, I could see the black waters of the ocean lapping at the beach, thin lines of foam delineating the waves. The moon was higher now, casting a bright irregular stripe onto the water's surface.

Time for a reality check, I thought.

"I'll be straight with you. If it weren't for your condition, I probably wouldn't even be here," I said. "But I'm here now. And he's not. So maybe we should think about other options?"

She said nothing.

"I can give you a lift to the bus station," I said. "Or, if you live a reasonable distance from here, a ride to that place."

"I can't go home," she said. "I've got no home to go to."

Great, I thought.

"Well, I've got work to do," I said. "I'll give you a lift back to town."

"He'll be here," she said. She affected a cool look. "Go. I'll be fine."

"Are you kidding? In your condition?"

"I wish you'd quit going on about that."

I would have to talk her into going back to Ocean City, I thought. Some place where she could get help, if she needed it. As I gazed out the window, something caught my eye, in the cattails.

"Hey, I see a car," I said. "A jeep, I think."

She made a stifled cry. I turned and got a brief glimpse of a man and a raised gun. Felt the shock of the gun connecting with my head. My knees buckled and, as they say in the old detective movies, everything went black.

φ

Voices and squeaking. And darkness. Eventually, I realized that was because my eyes were closed. Inside my head, a gnome in spike-heeled shoes was rhythmically kicking my skull. I tried to move my arms. They were pinned behind my back. My face was flattened against something. My whole right side, actually. The floor. I was on the floor, and the squeaking came from the floorboards, as people walked about.

"What do we do about her?" A young man's voice.

"What's there to do? We leave her." The girl.

"I don't know, Kaitlyn. What if she's with the DEA?"

"Don't you think she'd have some I.D. on her if she was with the DEA?"

"Not necessarily. Not if she's working undercover. Maybe she was sitting outside Eddie's place for a reason."

"Are you crazy?"

I opened my eyes, just a crack. I'd fallen behind the table and chairs. Through the legs, I had a pretty good view of them both–what I could see in the yellowish light between squinted lids, that is. The boy had a chunky, Junior Varsity build, and buzz cut hair. He walked around the room, making superfluous gestures as he spoke. The girl— Kaitlyn—had one hand on her hip and a look of disbelief on her face.

"You really fucked up, bringing her here," he said.

"Exactly how long was I supposed to wait for you, Trav?"

"I told you. The jeep's busted."

"And I was supposed to—what?—take a bus? If I were you, I'd be more worried about Eddie. By now, I'm sure he's figured out that I took some of his stuff."

Travis didn't seem convinced. "I dunno."

"Travis," Kaitlyn said, sounding more than a bit anxious. "Let's take the car, let's drive to the airport, and let's get the hell out of here, before Eddie figures out where we are."

"Do you know how much hard time you can do these days for drugs? Just for drugs! You can do life. Did you know that? Federal sentencing guidelines, babe. They're a bitch."

That seemed to stun her a little. "But they don't care about people like us. Besides, I don't think she's with the feds."

"So why was she waiting at the motel?"

"I dunno." She paused. "I never asked. But, for Christ sake, she's not a cop."

"So how would you know?"

"Cause she would have arrested me or something by now, stupid."

"For what, stupid?"

"You tell me. You're the one who's so sure she's a narc."

While they argued, I was quietly working at the rope around my wrists, using one of my fingernails to loosen the knot. It was a frustrating exercise, trying to work the knot and keep from moving too much. Fortunately, they weren't paying attention and the furniture blocked their view of me.

Travis bit a thumbnail. "Maybe I should just shut her up for good."

"Travis! Jesus!" She stared at him, eyes crazy with fear. "This woman saved my life. Besides, they may get me for drugs, but I'm not doing time for murder!"

He snorted. "Hell, Kate, you'd probably do *less* time."

He took a gun out of his waistband and turned it over in his hands a few times, as if he were trying to figure out how to use it. My armpits suddenly gushed sweat and my guts turned to liquid. I worked harder at the ropes, but it was going to take time. So many guns and so few brains, I thought. Humphrey Bogart. *The Maltese Falcon.* Stop thinking about old movies, you moron, and start coming up with ways to beg for your life. Because it looked like that's what I'd be doing in a few seconds.

But Kaitlyn had other ideas.

"No, Travis," she said. "No way!"

She grabbed for the gun. As they struggled, I kept working at the knot. The gun dropped to the floor. Suddenly, the door flew in, hitting the wall with a bang. The two of them jumped. A man rushed in—the blond man from the motel—and grabbed Kaitlyn, holding her arm behind her back with one hand and a gun to her head with the other. He kicked the door shut behind him.

The man smiled, a baring of teeth that was anything but humorous and that deepened the scar that ran from cheekbone to jaw on the left side of his face. His eyes were light gray. They looked as cold and pitiless as shark eyes.

Gesturing at the gun on the floor, he said, "Kick it here."

Travis hesitated. The man scowled and pulled back the hammer on his gun. As he jammed the barrel against Kaitlyn's head, she whimpered involuntarily.

Looking resigned, Travis shoved the gun with his foot toward the blond, who stooped to pick it up. As he rose, he suddenly lunged against Kaitlyn, shoving her, belly-first, into a nearby wall so quickly she had no time to cry out. She hit with a sickening crack that took the air out of my lungs and crumpled to the floor, holding herself protectively.

"Bastard," Travis muttered.

"Excuse me, what?" the blond said, in a voice both calm and menacing. "You steal my shit and I'm the bastard?"

His restless gaze swept the room and returned to them. "Who's that?" he asked Travis, gesturing vaguely toward me.

"Some broad."

"So what's her part?"

"She's not involved, Eddie," Kaitlyn said. "She was just there."

"Huh. That's handy. Don't look all that handy now, does she?" Again, he gestured with the gun. "Turn around. Put your hands to the wall. And don't fucking move."

Travis complied. Kaitlyn was still on the floor, frozen in place. Keeping his eyes on Travis, Eddie grabbed Kaitlyn by one ankle. She yelped as he yanked her, on her back, to the middle of the room.

"Hey!" Travis cried.

"Shut up!" Eddie shouted back. Travis glowered. I continued my slow work on the ropes. I was starting to make some headway now.

Eddie got on his knees between Kaitlyn's legs. Jesus, was he going to rape a pregnant woman? But then, something was odd. Something about that loud crack when she hit the wall, stomach-first.

Eddie threw up Kaitlyn's dress. Something like a plastic bowl was underneath, held in place with straps. Eddie undid the straps and removed the bowl. It contained a burlap sack. From the sack, Eddie pulled out four plastic bags of a white substance. Heroin, maybe.

As Eddie put the goods back in the sack, he said to Kaitlyn, "All right, you get up by the wall, too. Now."

Kaitlyn got up slowly and stood beside Travis.

"Face the wall like him," he ordered. "Then, both of you kneel down."

"Eddie...don't," Travis said.

"You've got your stuff," Kaitlyn said. Her voice shook with fear.

"And that's it, huh? I take my shit and let bygones be bygones? I think not."

"Eddie, please!" Kaitlyn started to cry. Travis looked like he was about to. Under his jeans, I could see the muscles in his legs quiver spastically.

"Believe me, it's so much easier this way," Eddie said. His voice was matter of fact, like that of a doctor discussing surgical options with a patient. "A bullet in the brain pan is a much easier death than a slug in the stomach. That's so...painful and takes so long." He grimaced in mock horror.

I had worked the knot loose and the rope was coming undone. I prayed that the kids could hold out a bit longer.

Eddie wasn't willing to wait, though. This wasn't *Dr. No* or *Goldfinger*, where he was going to engage his victims in small talk or devise complicated ways to kill them that they could defeat.

"You have five seconds to face the wall and get on your knees," he said. "Or I kill you where you stand. And, I promise you, it will hurt."

Kaitlyn moaned and Travis started muttering something that sounded like a prayer or a mantra. The rope slipped from my wrists. Everyone was too involved in their own personal extremity to notice me as I crept around the furniture. When I got clear of it, I sprang to my feet and lunged for Eddie's gut. I was on him before he could react. We fell to the floor together. The gun dropped from his hand and slid a few feet from us. I scrambled for it.

Behind me, I heard grunting and scuffling. I grabbed the gun and rolled into a sitting position. Eddie and Travis were struggling with the other gun. It went off with a startling bang. Broken glass tinkled and darkness swallowed the room. I flattened to the floor and started to crawl, trying to get my bearings. I groped with one hand, trying to avoid the shards of glass, and held the gun with the other hand. Slowly, my eyes adjusted. I could see two shadows wrestle, black on black.

A widening crack of gray slashed through the darkness. It was Kaitlyn, slipping out the door, the bag in hand. "Travis!" she called out. "I've got the stuff!"

There was another shot. A low moan in the dark. A thud as something heavy hit the floor. And other shot. I scuttled toward Kaitlyn.

"Travis!" she yelled again.

"Just go!" I said. The gun went off again, blowing off a piece of the door. Kaitlyn fled down the steps, with me behind her. She ran toward the sandy road, while I waited at the bottom of the stairs, hidden in the shadows beneath the house. The door opened and Eddie stepped out. As he took aim at Kaitlyn, I whirled around to the foot of the stairs and fired twice. Eddie curled like a leaf and tumbled over the side. I ran over to him. He was dead.

I took his gun and dashed to my car for a flashlight, then up the steps, two at a time, to check on him. The flashlight's beam caught Travis, crumpled in a corner, half his brains on the wall. An entry wound, like a third eye, was on his forehead, and the expression on his ghostly face was one of mild surprise.

I went back down, calling Kaitlyn's name. I trudged up the road a short ways, but saw no one and heard nothing except the sound of waves pounding the shore.

As I walked back to the car, keys in hand, I heard a noise behind me, then felt a solid blow to the back of my head. Pain stabbed my already throbbing brain. Everything turned to grainy brown, with white spots, like an old movie. The ocean roar became an unbearable pounding. I struggled to stay conscious. The world spun, and I was on my back looking at the sky. The man in the moon stared back at me, a gawking spectator to my predicament. I could hear the car start. Darkness blotted out the moon's stare.

When I woke up, it was still dark. The car was gone. I was lying next to a large piece of driftwood. Kaitlyn had left me. I checked my fanny pack and my wallet was still there, money and credit cards still in it. Decent of her. I guess it was the least she could do, after I'd saved her life. Twice.

I walked part way back to Ocean City, hitched the rest. I went to the beach and watched dawn break over the ocean, the sky turning to mother-of-pearl streaked with salmon, where the sun poked up over aqua-blue waters. Finally, I made my way back to the Bayside Villas, Unit 8. Mendez answered my knock. I must have looked a sight. Her mouth dropped open, but I held up my hand to stem the flow of questions.

"It's a long story," I said.

"Never mind that," she snapped. "We got some bad news, girl."

I came in and closed the door behind me. The bed was untouched and the T.V. set was on, the sound muted. "Your concern touches me. I probably have a concussion or two. But don't let that worry you. What's the problem?"

She flounced over to the bed and perched on the end. Her slender legs, encased in purple capri pants, looked poised and ready to spring at a moment's notice.

"Our connection. We can forget about that big meet we had worked out."

I stared at her. My head was starting to pound again. It wasn't the ocean this time. The T.V. set was tuned to the news. She picked up the remote. A reporter was droning about bodies found in Delaware.

Mendez gestured at the screen. "Look at this. Ay. Here we are, only trying to maintain national security and all, and we gotta depend on Eddie, the two-bit drug runner from Philadelphia. What a waste."

The video showed a familiar beach house.

"Looks like the little shit got into a shooting match with someone." Mendez lit a cigarette. "Some guy in the house bought it, too. Piece of shit—all of them. Fuck it. You have breakfast yet?"

I didn't answer right away. I watched the two bodies being carried from the stilted beach house.

φφφ

Debbi Mack is a freelance writer who practiced law in a previous life. Her novel, *Identity Crisis*, features female lawyer Sam McRae in a hardboiled mystery of murder and identity theft. Debbi has also written for newspapers, trade periodicals, reference books, legal publications and one of the Dow Jones newswires. A Queens, NY native, she is an avid reader, movie buff and baseball fan. Debbi, her husband and their family of four cats live in Columbia, Maryland.

SARAH'S STORY
by Jean McMillen

    Jo-Ann was Mamaw's youngest child, and at age 34 she was still her baby. Jo-Ann lived in Florida now but at the end of every visit home to Tennessee, she cried when she had to leave. Mamaw would never leave Tennessee. Once I mentioned I would like to see Paris, and she asked if I meant Paris, Tennessee.

    Mamaw's life was confined by geography but her imagination was out of this world, so I wasn't surprised when she told me my Aunt Jo-Ann was being stalked. Jo-Ann was my Daddy's little sister, and although she was twice my age we were more sisters than aunt and niece. She bridged the generation between my mother and me, and was the source of girl information in ways my mother couldn't be. It was Jo-Ann who taught me about hair and makeup and sex.

I was spending the summer with Mamaw and Papaw, my dad's parents. It was a hot August day and I was feeling drowsy from the sun and the heavy lunch Mamaw had cooked.

We were on the back porch shelling peas for supper and watching for Papaw to come home from the fields. This patch of East Tennessee was an oasis in the middle of development and subdivisions and tract houses all looking like a model house that had been cloned and the cloning had gotten out of hand.

I threw some peas into the bowl on Mamaw's lap. I said, "What do you mean, being stalked?"

Mamaw put her hands in her lap and looked off into the distance like the fields had an answer. She sighed and said, "Jo-Ann called me this morning. Said she was scared, some boy at the factory was following her around and calling her on the phone and then hanging up." Any man who dated any of Mamaw's three girls would always be a boy.

I laughed. "Mamaw, boys have been following Jo-Ann around for years."

Mamaw looked at me, sorrow on her face but fire in her eyes. "Yes, but they didn't scare her. I'm worried about her, Sarah, and I don't know what to do."

"Maybe she should come home for a while," I said. "Maybe he'll forget about her."

Mamaw nodded. "I think I'll see if she can get some time off and come home." She patted my knee. "You're a smart girl, Sarah."

The night Jo-Ann came home, I was sitting on the front porch worrying about my mom and dad.

Their fights were getting worse and I was afraid they'd divorce and I'd have to choose. I didn't know what to do. I loved them equally. It was barely dark and the cicadas were a Greek chorus to my worries.

Jo-Ann drove up in a hurry, got out of the car and shrieked. "He's still after me."

Mamaw grabbed her and still holding on, said, "Come inside, child. What's happened?"

Between sobs Jo-Ann said, "I thought I saw his van on the Interstate, but I couldn't be sure. Then when I stopped for gas he pulled into the station. I know it was him."

Papaw came into the front room looking ready for a fight. He grabbed Jo-Ann and gave her a big bear hug.

She said, "Oh, Daddy, I don't know what to do. I only went out with him a few times and now he won't leave me alone."

Papaw gently pulled Jo-Ann onto the sofa and sat next to her. Mamaw went out to the kitchen for iced tea. Papaw said, "Now, don't you worry. If that boy comes around here, I'll give him something to worry about." He looked across the room at his gun cabinet.

When Jo-Ann had calmed down, Papaw brought her suitcase inside, and we all talked about her problem until we were sleepy and ready for bed. Most evenings Mamaw, Papaw and I sat on the porch, but tonight we needed the safety of four walls.

Upstairs in my bedroom, a loft overlooking fields and trees, I wondered about Jo-Ann's stalker. For a second I imagined I could see him running toward the house. Then I calmed down, turned on my bedside lamp and crawled into bed. I read myself to sleep with *Shattered Silk* by Barbara Michaels, a delicious mystery set in Georgetown, DC.

I slept like a baby, and the next morning the aroma of coffee found its way upstairs and got me up. I grabbed a pair of shorts and a shirt off the floor and went downstairs. Mamaw, Papaw, and Jo-Ann were at the kitchen table looking grim.

"I think we need to call the sheriff," Mamaw said. She put her coffee cup down on the table. She had a "don't mess with me" look in her eyes.

Papaw shook his head and said, "No call for that. He couldn't do nothing."

"There's nothing anybody can do," said Jo-Ann. She stood up. She looked at me and said, "Morning, Sarah. I'm glad to see you." She gave me a hug, then said, "I'm going upstairs to get dressed."

I poured myself a cup of coffee and sat down at the table. I asked, "So what are we going to do?" No one seemed to want to come out and say it, but as much as we all loved her, we knew Jo-Ann was a bit of a ditz. I knew we were all thinking maybe she was exaggerating a little. Oh, sure, she thought she was being stalked, but I personally wouldn't have ruled out a little misinterpretation on her part. I listened to Mamaw and Papaw debate getting help for Jo-Ann and protection from her stalker while I ate bacon and eggs. When I finished my breakfast, they were still going around in the same circle.

Jo-Ann came back to the kitchen and said, "I want to go shopping." She had put on white shorts and a bright, tight yellow T and designer sandals. Her legs were tanned and shiny like they had been polished. If she was trying to go unnoticed, it wasn't working.

I told Jo-Ann I'd go shopping with her. Papaw left for the fields and Mamaw went out to work in her vegetable garden.

On the way to the shopping mall, Jo-Ann drove like a maniac, swinging around stiff curves and over ruts in the road like she was in a race for her life. When we got to I-81 she gunned her car and kept pace with the trucks, waving to them with a little flutter of her fingers. With her bleached white hair and short shorts, I thought she looked like an extra in an old Grade B movie. My blond hair and skinny legs made me feel like a modern-day star, maybe Britney Spears.

In my peripheral vision I kept seeing a gray SUV followed by a green Honda Civic. Were they following us? I pushed the thought of my head. No point in getting paranoid.

At Bristol Mall we wandered around, looking at but not buying the pretty but pricey dresses and shoes. The day was nearly over and although we had eaten our way around the mall—popcorn, fast-food pizza, and ice cream—I couldn't say no when Jo-Ann asked if I wanted to go to the Cracker Barrel for supper.

Over fried chicken, macaroni and cheese, and collard greens, Jo-Ann told me about her stalker. Bo was a country boy who had settled in Jacksonville. He and Jo-Ann had met at the paper plant and gone out a few times but then Jo-Ann met someone else and told Bo she didn't want to go out with him again. Right away he turned nasty.

"What do you mean, nasty?" I asked.

"Well, loud—shouted at me, threatened me, said nobody was going to mess with his girl. It was scary."

"How did you get rid of him?"

"I yelled back, gave him Mamaw's evil eye and told him to get out. I think it shocked him so I was able to sort of push him out the door and lock it."

"Had you seen any of this behavior before? At work, maybe?"

Jo-Ann shook her head. "No, he was sweet as could be. That's why I told him the truth—I wanted to be nice." She shuddered. "Wow, did he turn 180 degrees."

"What does this guy look like? I think I need to know." I looked around the restaurant. It was crowded at suppertime, with a lot of overweight people looking like maybe they'd gain another few pounds tonight, judging by what they had on their plates. The Cracker Barrel was a country restaurant and served basic ham, meat loaf, pork chops, potatoes, greens, and beans. I didn't see anyone who matched Jo-Ann's description of a tall, thin, blond, good-looking guy.

By the time we finished eating, it was nearly nine o'clock and completely dark. We headed out on the Interstate, listening to the radio and summer night sounds. We were relaxed, off guard, when an SUV came up behind us in a hurry. The headlights flooded the inside of Jo-Ann's car. She looked over at me and said, "What in the world?"

Then the SUV bumped us and Jo-Ann swerved but got control of the car. My heart swerved with the car. A second later, the SUV bumped us again but this time Jo-Ann had both hands tight on the wheel and we felt the bump but stayed on the road. Then the SUV suddenly whipped out beside us and going way over the speed limit, was gone.

Jo-Ann and I looked at each other, with fear in our eyes and our hearts in our mouths.

I spoke first. "Your stalker?"

"That bastard! Who does he think he is? That was no stalking. That's harassment."

"I agree. That van meant business. What did he want?"

"What he got—he hassled us. He scared us."

"And what about the car that pulled out right behind him?" When my heart had left my mouth and found its way back to my chest, I remembered seeing a Honda Civic speeding behind the SUV. It reminded me of the two cars I had seen earlier. Maybe I wasn't being paranoid.

"I don't know. Do you think they were together? A stalking caravan?"

"Gosh, I don't know. Do you think we should we report this?"

"I think we should."

I looked across the darkened car. Jo-Ann looked back at me.

"But we won't," I said.

Jo-Ann nodded. "It might get worse if we fight back."

We drove home very carefully.

"You are too reporting this." Papaw had his hand on the phone, ready to call the sheriff.

"Oh, Daddy, what good will it do?" Jo-Ann whined away the suggestion. Oblivious to caffeine, we were all drinking Coke classic. I wasn't sure my body would calm down enough to sleep tonight anyway.

Papaw looked determined. "Good or not, that bastard can't get away with this."

"We don't know if it was him." I said, sounding more mature than I felt.

Mamaw was almost as hysterical as Jo-Ann on the night she got here. She said, "What difference does it make if it was him or somebody else. It happened."

"It matters that we report this stalking business." Papaw hushed when the sheriff answered the phone.

When the incident was reported and Papaw was satisfied he had done all he could, we spent the next couple of hours sitting around the kitchen table rehashing the conversation we had had the night Jo-Ann came home.

The sheriff called the next morning while Mamaw, Jo-Ann, and I were canning tomatoes. He had run a check on Bo and told us the police were looking for him—a couple of years ago he had beat his wife, put her in the hospital, and had skipped town. Turns out he had lived right here in East Tennessee, about 100 miles away. My first thought was maybe he wasn't stalking Jo-Ann the night she got here. Maybe he was just sneaking home. Then I remembered the SUV and canceled that thought. I think Jo-Ann must have been thinking how that bad boy had seemed so good.

A few days passed and nothing more happened—no word on Bo, no stalking, no late night incidents, and Jo-Ann was thinking about going home. She and I decided to cook Mamaw and Papaw a nice Sunday dinner before she left. On Saturday morning we drove over to Kroger's to get groceries.

Jo-Ann parked the car and when we got out I was enjoying the late summer sun on my face when I heard Jo-Ann hiss with a sharp intake of breath.

She said, "Bo, you bastard. Get away from me."

A nice looking, tall, blond-haired man had grabbed Jo-Ann's hand. She jerked away and said, "Get lost."

I looked around for help but at midmorning the parking lot was in a lull and no one was around. I didn't want to leave Jo-Ann and I didn't want to scare Bo by yelling for help. I stood there, feeling helpless.

Bo said, "I've been watching you. You can't get away from me. You're my girl." He staggered a little and I could smell liquor on his breath. Jo-Ann tried to step aside. From a distance they looked like they could have been dancing. It seemed like five minutes but it couldn't have been more than a few seconds before there was a sound like a car backfiring, and Bo lost his balance completely and fell backward on the pavement. I realized the backfire must have been a shot when I saw blood oozing on the parking lot.

Suddenly people appeared from all directions, running and asking what happened. Jo-Ann looked like she was about to faint so I took her over to a bench in front of the grocery store and she sat with her head between her knees. I saw the action in front of us like a movie. I rubbed Jo-Ann's back while I watched the ambulance arrive and load Bo into it. I thought in the confusion Jo-Ann and I could just slip away but my sense of ethics and justice kept us sitting there.

After a while Ivan, the sheriff's deputy, walked over and asked us if we knew anything. In as few words as possible, we told him about Bo stalking Jo-Ann and being wanted by the police. We knew when he talked to the sheriff he'd have the full story on Bo. We called Papaw to come and pick us up because neither of us was in any shape to drive.

Bo died in the ambulance on the way to the hospital. No one knew who had shot him or why, but Jo-Ann's problem was over. That Sunday Mamaw cooked dinner. Jo-Ann and I were too upset and besides we never did buy those groceries. Mamaw made chicken and dumplings, green beans, sliced cantaloupe and tomatoes from the garden, and served them with her baked biscuits, mashed potatoes, and fried apple pies. We drank a gallon of iced tea.

The next morning Jo-Ann left for Florida and in a few days I went back home to start my last year of high school. That seemed like the end of the story.

But unlike art life can be messy and doesn't always come with clear beginnings and endings. At Christmas that year Mom, Dad, and I went to Mamaw's and Papaw's for the holidays. While I was worrying about them during the summer, they had been to counseling and were getting along fine. In October I had met the love of my life (so far) and this would be the first time we would be apart. He was blond and cute and sweet. I wondered if Bo had been like that, in the beginning, for his wife and for Jo-Ann, and I thought how hard it is for women to leave a good man gone bad, how we keep hoping to find the boy we used to know.

Jo-Ann drove up from Florida with her friend Kathy who was visiting friends nearby. On Christmas

Eve Jo-Ann and I drove over to Kathy's friend's apartment to a party. The music was loud and the booze was flowing. Kathy introduced us to the hosts, the young couple she was visiting. Kathy and Jo-Ann had worked together at the paper mill but Jo-Ann had gotten another job—too many unhappy memories, and even though Bo was dead, Jo-Ann still hadn't gotten over it.

Kathy introduced us around and Jo-Ann and I ended up in the dining room. We got drinks and looked over the food on the buffet table. A thin, middle-aged woman was munching chips. She had a glass of white wine in her hand and if her eyes were any indication, it wasn't her first of the evening.

"Nice party," Jo-Ann said—the social butterfly.

The woman had a hard face and stiff blond hair. "Hi. It is nice." She squinted a little. "Are you friends of Tim and Sandy?" It took a minute for me to remember they were our hosts.

Jo-Ann picked up a chip and popped it in her mouth. "We're friends of friends. I'm Jo-Ann and this is my niece Sarah. We're from out of town."

The blonde put out her hand and said, "Pleased to meet you. I'm Sis Anderson." Her voice sounded like too many late nights and too many cigarettes. A young couple walked in and I decided to slip out to the powder room. Out of the corner of my eye I saw Sis leave the room, too.

I met Kathy in the hall and snagged directions to the powder room. I was standing at the sink washing my hands when I heard two women talking, as clear as if they were in the room with me. I looked up and realized the voices were coming from an air vent in the wall. The women must have been in a bedroom nearby.

"I think she's the woman Bo was following around."

"I think so, too. She's the one he was with when he was shot." I recognized Sis Anderson's throaty voice. I didn't recognize the other one.

"Does she know Clarice was following her and stalking her and Bo both?"

"God knows. Clarice didn't make any secret about tailing them in her Honda Civic."

"But Clarice had been after Bo for years, ever since she got out of the hospital and the sheriff wasn't looking too hard for him."

"How did she happen to find him anyway?"

"Oh, quite by accident. She spotted him in town one day and followed him everywhere he went after that. She chased him the night he went after Jo-Ann in the SUV, nearly caught him with her Honda. She probably saved Jo-Ann's life, and that niece of hers, too. Anyway, she followed him for days, not sure what she wanted to do with him. Then she was at the photo shop across the mall keeping an eye on him when she saw him struggling with Jo-Ann. That's when she lost it. She just took a chance and pulled out her gun."

"But how did she know he'd die? She sure took a chance."

"She didn't care. She just felt good about hitting him, the way he had hit her."

"How long were they married?"

"A few years. Long enough."

"And if she hadn't killed him?"

"It didn't matter to her. It was instinct that she didn't want to see him hit another woman. She knew she was dying. The cancer had already spread, and she knew it was just a matter of time."

"God bless her. Have you been back to her grave?"

"Not since Thanksgiving. It's hard to say good-bye to a baby sister."

I had heard enough. I slipped out the door and went back to the party. I met Jo-Ann in the living room. She looked tired and ready to go home.

I was quiet in the car on the way home, thinking about the conversation I never should have heard. I never told Jo-Ann, or anybody. Some point out that the word listen has the same letters as the word silent, and that's what I decided to be. Later on I heard the sheriff had closed the case. I guess the lesson for me was THE END only happens in books or the movies—in real life you never know for sure when it's the end of the story.

φφφ

Jean McMillen is a lifelong mystery reader and fan and the founder/owner of the former Mystery Bookshop in Bethesda, Maryland. She and her husband Ron served on the board of Malice Domestic for many years and compiled and wrote *Cooking with Malice Domestic*, a real cookbook with recipes from 58 mystery authors. She is a health educator and published author and is currently working at a large public relations agency in Washington DC. She is also working on a novel.

THE CASA GRANDE
by Nancy Nelson

I was at the Casa Grande in Managua the only time I met Elena Torres, and what I have learned since then has not made me inclined to like her any more now than I had then. It was a nasty way to die, but she was a nasty lady. Still, it surprised me. I've become accustomed to the drawn-out negotiations and the lengthy ministerials that are the hallmark of my business; violence in the tropics erupts suddenly, then dies out just as quickly. The excitement surrounding Elena's murder didn't even last long enough to disturb the hot, sticky air of Managua.

My job at the embassy had kept me late; the reception had been going for nearly an hour by the time I arrived at the Casa Grande. The event was being held in honor of a group of 23 property claimants from Miami. Their property had been expropriated by the Sandinistas when Somoza was thrown out, and now that a new government had come into office, they were trying to get it back. The room was thronged with people; embassy staff members, Nicaraguan government officials, and the property claimants themselves. The elegantly dressed crowd mingled under the chandeliers, their subdued conversation blending in smoothly with the music of a small salsa band playing in the background. Waiters darted back and forth like silent black dragonflies, filling up drink glasses and picking up used plates.

The one jarring note was the woman who had Craig Jenkins, the embassy's property officer, backed up against a wall. They were at least twenty feet away, but the woman's blaring, abrasive voice was attracting a crowd.

"Don't tell me you're working on it! My tax dollars pay for your salary so you'd better get this done!"

The woman's face was twisted in anger, but I could still see she was good-looking, maybe in her early thirties. She was clad in a tight yellow dress that showed off more, rather than less of her figure, and her hair was that brassy burgundy color that black hair sometimes turns when it's dyed red. She was about the same height as Craig, but bristling in anger she loomed taller.

Craig said something quietly to the woman that I didn't catch. This only seemed to make things worse.

"I don't think you realize who my friends are," she hissed. "You'll regret this." Then she turned and stalked away—a fiery yellow blaze parting the crowd.

Chatter rose up around me as people turned from the scene back to their conversations. I strolled over to where Craig was still standing looking shaken. "I don't know who her friends are," I said. "Should I?"

"Hi, Liza." His voice was weary. "You've just had the pleasure of meeting Elena Torres, my unhappiest customer."

"She's a little young to be a property claimant, isn't she?" The delegation's average age was nearly 70.

"It's actually her parents' claim; Elena was only a child when the Sandinistas expropriated her family's property. She's acting on their behalf."

"Lucky you." A passing waiter paused with a tray of wine classes. I exchanged my now-empty glass for another of red. Craig took a glass of white.

"We're doing everything we can!" he said. "It's just not so simple. After her parents' property was taken away, it was divided into small plots and given to landless peasants. These people have lived on this land for 15 years; they've built houses on it and farmed it. And they're just this close to being destitute." Craig held up his hand with thumb and forefinger pinched tightly together and shook it in my face for emphasis.

I took a sip of my wine and watched the crowd. The music had gotten louder—it was a rumba now—and several couples had gotten up to dance. I didn't see Elena.

"Most people have been willing to wait the year or two that it takes these people to find someplace else to live," continued Craig, almost to himself. "But not Elena. She has no patience; she wants everything immediately and she screams and yells at people to get it."

"She's not so bad when you get to know her," said a voice from one side.

Both Craig and I turned to stare in surprise at Terri, the Casa Grande's manager. Balancing two trays of food in her hands, she appeared to be on her way to the hors d'oeuvres table.

"You've found time to have a heart-to-heart with her?" I said.

I shouldn't have been surprised. Although it wasn't in her job description, the tall, gregarious Terri acted as an unofficial welcoming committee for anyone visiting the Casa Grande.

Terri just smiled, "She's not so bad," and continued across the room.

In retrospect, that was both the first and last good thing I ever heard anyone say about Elena Torres.

φ

I don't like blood much, I'm just curious. So when David, the embassy's consular officer, joined the small crowd of people standing atop the hill behind the Intercontinental Hotel, I went with him. But one glance was enough and I turned quickly away. I wasn't even supposed to be there, but the police didn't object. Being a diplomat, I can get into things that I shouldn't.

David had been giving me a ride to work that morning when his cell phone rang with the report of a dead American. Of course he went straight to the scene. Although I was only there by chance—an interloper—I was the first to speak.

"I wonder who Elena pissed off?" I said, feeling slightly queasy as I turned away from the sight.

"You know her?" said David, joining me. A strong, hot wind full of sand and grit was blowing up from the valley, forcing our eyes to narrow slits.

Even through the blood, the yellow dress and brassy hair were unmistakable. The body was sprawled face-up behind a low concrete wall incongruously located at the foot of a forty-foot tall billboard featuring the Nicaraguan revolutionary Sandino.

I nodded. "Elena Torres is a property claimant with the Miami delegation. I met her last night at the Casa Grande."

A few Nicaraguan policemen were busy securing the area and keeping back the curiosity seekers who were already milling about. To one side, a plainclothes detective was interviewing a shaken-looking young man in a bellhop's uniform. He had spotted the body on his way to work at the Intercontinental Hotel—referred to simply as "the Intercon" by the locals—and raised the alarm.

David turned away to talk business with a senior-looking police officer so I let my gaze wander over the tropical landscape and down the dirt road that led to the Intercontinental Hotel where the Miami delegation was staying. I took a deep breath to settle my stomach, but the hot, heavy air didn't refresh.

I was curious about what had happened. While Elena could have walked from the Intercon, I doubt she would have tried it while wearing heels and a tight dress. Not on an unpaved road and in the dark. And a murder at the foot of the Sandino billboard was bizarre. Why had Elena even come here? It wasn't a popular nighttime destination; the area was too isolated.

I started as David tapped my shoulder. "Since you met the victim before, the police would like to ask you a couple of questions."

The chubby policeman had an impressive moustache à la Hercule Poirot, but that's where the resemblance ended; his questions were perfunctory at best. I was asked to confirm Elena's identity, state when I had last seen her, and account for my whereabouts—all the things you see on old cop shows in the U.S. When my interrogator didn't appear very interested in the answers I gave, I asked a question of my own.

"How did she die?"

The policeman looked up at me as if I was an idiot. "She was stabbed, Senorita Heywood."

He was right. The knife wounds were obvious.

"But what was she doing here?" I said. I pointed to a small leather handbag peeking out from below the sprawled body. "It wasn't robbery."

"We must make an inventory of her purse before we make that decision, Senorita." He shrugged his shoulders unimaginatively. "Probably she was here with a man."

Funny. Elena hadn't struck me as the kind of woman who would be making romantic assignations in isolated spots. She seemed to care too much about herself to do that.

If I had cared as much about myself, I would have left it at that.

φ

The ride to the Casa Grande later that afternoon was a quiet one. David was doing the driving again, and his silent treatment let me know that he was unhappy that I was coming along. It was consular business, after all, and since I deal only with economic issues, I shouldn't have been there. But that wasn't a sufficient reason when my employee's brother was arrested.

"He didn't do it, Liza, he couldn't have!" Emilio had burst into my office in distress just a couple of hours earlier.

He was talking about the murder of Elena Torres, of course. Emilio's brother Hector lived on part of the property being claimed by Elena Torres' parents. Earlier the previous day Elena and Hector had had a screaming match—Elena had threatened to come back accompanied by a police squad to forcibly evict Hector and his family from their home. That night several employees at the Intercontinental Hotel had seen Hector enter the lobby and go into the elevator. Hector himself had admitted to seeing her that night, and even to having had a second heated discussion in her hotel room.

"He thought he could get her to change her mind," Emilio had explained.

And when Hector realized she wouldn't change her mind, he somehow lured her up the hill to the Sandino billboard and then stabbed her, I thought to myself. But even as the possibility crossed my mind I dismissed it. Why not just stab Elena in her room? The only reason for taking her to another spot to kill her was to avoid being seen; Hector's visit hadn't been a secret.

"I'll see what I can do," I had promised Emilio.

I spent a good hour regretting those words as David lectured to me on how it was better to avoid getting involved and to leave these things to the police. I listened dutifully, but in the end David had agreed to let me go with him to the Casa Grande where the Nicaraguan police wanted to interview the remaining Miami delegation members. I didn't think they would object to my being there even though I didn't belong. Maybe my calm and impartial attitude would help. After all, I was a diplomat.

The Casa Grande is a gleaming white, hacienda-style mansion situated on a hill overlooking all of Managua, and is the former residence of a long line of U.S. ambassadors to Nicaragua. For decades its grandiose design and beautifully landscaped grounds were deemed necessary for the American image; invitations to the U.S. ambassadors' parties were the most sought after in town. That ended when the Sandinistas came into power and diplomatic security dictated that a lower profile residence be located. But with its palm trees and white columns and panoramic view of Managua, the Casa Grande was still used for official functions like the reception I had attended the previous evening.

This was probably the first time it had been used for a police interrogation.

David and I arrived at the Casa Grande a few minutes after the property claimants. The staff had settled the Miamians in a sunroom, and was doing its best to pretend this was just another social occasion.

The Casa Grande manager, Terri, was making sure that everyone had coffee or tea, and directing waiters as they walked around offering small sandwiches on trays. I pulled her aside.

"So, how are things going?"

"Not too badly; since the police have already arrested someone, questioning this group seems to be just for appearances." Terri ran her hand through her blond hair and looked critically out over the room. The Miami delegation members were seated in small groups chatting quietly amongst themselves. "Everything's going fine so far."

Terri was an efficient manager; the Casa Grande was lucky to have her. An expatriate American, she had settled in Managua a decade earlier after meeting and marrying a local boy while doing the rain forest thing. Her husband's sudden death of a heart attack a few years later had unexpectedly left her to provide for herself and their young daughter, and she had applied for the job of Casa Grande manager. Now no one could imagine life at the embassy without her.

"Where are the interviews taking place?"

Terri nodded her head towards a dark wooden door in the hallway. "In the library. Go on in if you want."

I didn't bother. Instead I stayed in the sunroom listening to the property claimants eagerly chat about the experience.

"She came from a good family," said an overweight lady as she sipped her tea. She was sitting with three other elderly delegation members in rattan chairs arranged around a low glass table. The sun was shining in brightly, but the shade from nearby potted ferns and an overhead fan gave the area a cool feeling. I sat down in an empty chair next to them.

"So you knew Elena before you came on this trip?" I asked, turning to the woman who had been speaking.

"We all knew Elena before this trip, dear." She reached over and patted my hand comfortingly. "And we all know each other. Not before the Sandinistas came, of course, but we've all been working on this same property issue these last ten years and Miami isn't that big."

The other three people around the table, two women and a man, nodded.

"The news is going to be a blow to her parents," she fretted. "They made such an effort with her, and now this."

"Elena was a little on the wild side during her college years," explained another woman who was bent over some crocheting. "She got in with a bad crowd. But after her parents pulled her out of a couple of tight spots, she settled down. No trouble at all."

The other elderly people around the table nodded again.

"She didn't seem very polite," I said frankly. "I know that she threatened the suspect who the police arrested, and I heard her threaten the embassy's property officer last night at the reception."

The others considered my statement with equanimity. "Well she didn't have many friends," conceded the lady who was crocheting. "She had an abrasive way about her."

"But she was a looker," offered up the lone man. He drained the last drops of coffee from his cup and looked around for more. Ever vigilant, Terri hurried over with a heavy silver coffee pitcher.

"Beauty is as beauty does," said the overweight lady. "She would have been more attractive if she had smiled at people more often—and did something to moderate that voice of hers."

"She was too vain to do that," said Terri under her breath, apparently to herself, as she poured the coffee. I wanted to ask her about it, but just then someone from the next table asked about getting a refill of tea and she turned away. Then David and the policemen came out of the library, evidently finished with their questioning.

I helped the Casa Grande staff herd the Miami delegation back to their bus as David tied up some loose ends with the police. It was hot and sticky out. David and I watched the two groups leave, then got into his car.

"Did anything new turn up?" I asked, swabbing at the sweat on my neck with a tissue.

"Nothing," said David. He adjusted the rear view mirror and began to back up out of his parking space. "Emilio is going to be disappointed. His brother is guilty."

I didn't say anything. There was no other explanation. I moved David's briefcase so that I could buckle my seat belt. There was a ladies leather handbag underneath it.

"The police gave you Elena's purse?" I said.

"They're done with it; I have to send it back to the U.S. with her other belongings."

I opened the handbag and started rummaging through it; a mirror, two lipstick tubes, a comb, a bottle of bright red nail polish, and a little plastic box.

I took out the box, turned it over, and flipped open the lid. Two small, oddly-shaped plastic objects fell into my hand.

David glanced over, "What are those?"

I stared down at my hand at first uncomprehendingly, then in growing excitement. "Pull over!"

Startled, David stopped the car. I jumped out and called back to David, "I'll just be a few minutes – I need to check something out."

I crossed the 50 yards back up the drive to the Casa Grande at a trot, pulled open the heavy front door of the mansion and stepped inside. "Terri!" I called out.

"In here!" came the muted reply. I crossed through the front reception area and into the sunroom where the property claimants had had their coffee. The staff had already removed most of the serving trays and dirty dishes to the back kitchen. Terri was alone as she finished cleaning up the room.

"I thought you were gone, Liza. Did you forget something?" She flashed a smile at me as she placed the silver coffee pitcher on a pushcart. I swallowed the lump in my throat.

"I just wanted to know how long you've known Elena Torres," I said quietly.

It looked like Terri paused for a brief moment, but that might have been my imagination.

"That woman who was murdered? I met her the other night at the reception just like you did." She turned to move a rattan chair back against a wall.

"But you had met her before that; you told me that she wasn't that bad after you got to know her."

"I didn't mean anything by it. At the beginning of the reception she came into the kitchen to complain about something, and after we talked for a few minutes she softened up. That's all." Terri took an ornamental pillow from a chair and plumped it up.

"But you knew her well; you knew that she was too vain to wear her hearing aids," I said even more quietly, holding out the plastic box so that she could see. "That's why her voice sounded so abrasive; she was hard of hearing."

Terri stared at my outstretched hand for a few brief moments, then her face crumpled. "She threatened me. She said that if I didn't pull strings to get her parents' property back she would go to the ambassador and get me fired." Her body sagged down into the chair.

"Elena was in college when it happened, right?" I said, remembering back to the comments of property claimants that afternoon.

"We were both in the same dorm. Everyone did drugs back then." Terri stared down at the floor as she talked, her voice toneless. "But Elena was out of control, really wild. After a couple of kids overdosed there was a sweep of the dorm; Elena was picked up."

"And she implicated you," I guessed.

"I wasn't a dealer, but if I got hold of more than I could use, I let other students buy it from me. I never sold anyone the hard stuff—I didn't even use it myself. But Elena named me as her supplier—she didn't want to incriminate her real source. Elena portrayed herself as someone who was helplessly addicted and at the mercy of the big, bad pusher—

me. Her parents pulled some strings and got her into treatment. But the university wanted to make an example of me." Terri's voice was bitter and her hands were clenching and unclenching convulsively. She continued: "The university did everything it could to get me a stiff sentence. I was just an average student, but they gave me six years."

"So you fled the country, ended up in Nicaragua, and made a new life for yourself. And everything was fine until Elena came along."

"She wanted me to pull strings in the American Embassy to get her parents' property back," said Terri, her voice rising incredulously. "When I told her that things didn't work that way she didn't believe me; she wouldn't listen. Elena said that if I didn't do something to get the property back within the next month she'd tell the ambassador about my arrest and get me sent back to the U.S." She abruptly rose up out of her chair and began to pace back and forth.

"So you arranged to meet her late last night at the Sandino billboard," I said, holding myself still as Terri paced by. While both Terri and Elena had done terrible things, I couldn't help but feel a small glow of very human self-satisfaction—I had managed to figure out something that had escaped even the police!

"She deserved it!" Terri said in anguish. "And I'm glad she's dead. If anyone had found out that I was a fugitive, the embassy would have fired me and had me extradited to the States. I've lived in Nicaragua for years; I have a daughter who depends on me. I couldn't let Elena ruin my life like that."

There are certain moments in everyone's life when suddenly you realize something that has probably been crystal clear to everyone else all along. It was at the moment when Terri stopped pacing and looked over at me that my feeling of self-satisfaction evaporated and I became conscious of just how stupid I had been to come back and confront Terri by myself.

"Liza," she said, coming forward slowly and her voice suddenly calm again, "you are really very clever."

My heart in my mouth, I backed up one or two steps, then whirled around to escape through the door. But Terri crossed the distance between us in just a few strides, grabbed on hard to my elbow with one hand, and circled her other arm around my neck. Terri's hold was like a vice.

"Liza," she said softly into my ear, "I'm so sorry." Her voice was sincere.

It wasn't until she began dragging me back into the room that I started struggling. I screamed and kicked out, but Terri's arms held me tight and she clamped a hand over my mouth. Throwing me down on one of the padded loveseats, Terri pressed her knee on my chest and forced down a pillow onto my face. I turned my head back and forth, my lungs bursting, desperate for air. It couldn't have been long before my struggles became weaker, and, after a time, finally ceased. My lungs no longer hurt; my mind was floating in an abyss.

It was a shock then, when Terri's weight suddenly lifted and sunlight flooded my eyes. I turned over, taking a few ragged breaths, then vomited on to the floor. When my eyes were able to focus again, I turned around and saw a white-faced David standing there with the pillow in one hand, the Casa Grande's heavy silver coffee pitcher in the other. Terri was lying at his feet.

"You were taking more than a few minutes," David explained in a tight, matter of fact voice, "so I came in."

φ

Terri's concussion wasn't fatal; she recovered enough to leave the hospital after two weeks, and, as she had predicted, was promptly extradited back to the States. I think her daughter was sent to live with relatives. It wasn't a happy situation.

There were other awkward things that I had to do, like explaining everything to the police, and trying to justify why I had gone back to confront Terri by myself rather than telling the authorities what I had found out. There really wasn't a reason that sounded sensible. We finally all agreed that the tropical heat sometimes causes American ladies to act foolishly.

The same could be said about Elena Torres. I've said before that she was a nasty lady, but she was also very foolish. Her murder didn't really surprise anyone. Except for me of course, and I shouldn't even have been involved. But then I get into things I shouldn't. I'm a diplomat.

φφφ

Nancy Nelson draws on her experience working as a U.S. diplomat to develop the settings and characters in her stories. Having completed tours in

Washington, Venezuela, Nicaragua and Estonia, Ms. Nelson is now assigned to Ottawa, Canada, where she lives with her two children and two cats.

POSSESSING MARTINE

by Judy Pomeranz

I recall how my pulse accelerated as the painting emerged from the packing materials. A delicate young man from the lower rungs of the curatorial staff of the lending institution—the National Gallery of Art—removed it from the shipping crate and lifted it onto an easel. Though he was deliberate and undeniably careful in his movements, I didn't feel he accorded the work or the event the dignity each deserved. I had waited an entire career for this moment.

All three of us, the young man, the black-clad female conservator and I, Michael Handley, curator, instinctively stepped back from the easel and stared silently at the painting. We pitched our heads at odd angles; we looked through squinted, then fully opened eyes. Then we began to edge sideways in a slow, finely choreographed pattern, shifting places with one another, taking the painting in from all possible perspectives. I caught a glimpse of the young man's face at one point in our little dance, and was disappointed to see his eyes filled not with ecstasy but analytical intensity. He didn't smile, he studied. It was a reaction I would have expected from the conservator, but not from an assistant curator—not from a man whose life, whose very world, revolved around these works of art, just as mine did.

I was the first to move forward; it was as if the others were waiting for my permission to come close. I stepped up to within a foot of the painting and leaned into it. I stared at the center, at that brilliant bit of lavender that highlighted the ribbons on the golden dress. The conservator shone a bright lamp on the painting, for which I nodded thanks without taking my gaze off the woman's breast. Then I moved my eyes, ever so slowly, in concentric circles of sight, around and around and around, covering each and every centimeter of canvas.

I admired the impasto touches, the virtuoso flourishes for which Fragonard is so well loved. I drank in the rich, saturated yellows, snowy white highlights, and those surprises of purple and blue one notices only when one stops to think about it. I tried, as I had so often before, to understand how the artist knew just exactly when to begin shading from one color into the next to create such a convincing illusion of lush texture, three dimensionality, and that wonderfully dewy skin of which just tiny, tantalizing bits were visible. I tried to comprehend how one could compose such an ethereal vision with the pedestrian tools of paint and brush. I gazed at the woman's hair and saw that, up close, under harsh light, it looked not at all like hair but like elegant flashes of color.

I studied the craquelure, those hair-fine lines running through the paint that resulted from too many years of shifting temperatures, barometric conditions, and locations. While it gave the painting a gentle, mellow quality never to be found in modern works, the craquelure troubled me because it stood as a reminder of the centuries that had passed since this unparalleled creature had walked the earth.

"Looks pretty good, huh?" the assistant curator said.

I had momentarily forgotten I was in the company of others.

"Pretty good?" I said. "That's the best you can say about this exquisite work of art?" I must have spoken more loudly than I intended, for the young man's head snapped up. He looked concerned, even chastened.

"I meant the condition," he said softly. "No visible damage in transit."

I saw him direct a quizzical look at the conservator. I could only imagine the disdain her return glance must have held, for I was quite accustomed to being ridiculed for my enthusiasm. For other things as well.

"Quite so," I acknowledged. "No visible damage."

φ

That moment—the unveiling and my first opportunity to scrutinize "A Young Girl Reading" at close hand and at leisure—will stay with me forever.

They can do what they will to me, take what they want from me, but no one can ever eliminate from my memory the moment when she came into my custody. Nor can they take away the weeks we lived together, weeks during which I memorized each and every brushstroke, each and every color, shape, line, and texture. Her skin, her hair, her attentive eyes, her soft, full figure and her demeanor of utter peace and contentment are engraved on my soul.

φ

"Brilliant," my thesis advisor had said. "This is a brilliant piece of scholarship." A broad smile illuminated his face. "I thought I knew all there was to know about Fragonard, but you've put me to shame. I now see the artist—and most certainly this painting—in an entirely new light."

I cast my eyes modestly down at the floor.

After an undistinguished academic career, first at Columbia, then at Yale, my doctoral thesis finally brought me the recognition I craved. I chose to examine a single painting, "A Young Girl Reading," from an unconventional perspective. I didn't try to find hidden symbolism in its iconography or reveal *pentimenti* that would indicate shifting aesthetic intentions on the part of the artist. I wasn't interested in the socio-economic environment in which it was painted or in how that environment was mirrored in the work. I didn't care to address or overrule earlier studies of technique or provenance. I wanted only, and quite simply, to discover who the subject was and why Fragonard chose to paint her as he did.

To judge from my thesis review committee's reaction, I had succeeded admirably in doing just that.

But I hadn't done it for them; it was an entirely personal quest. From the very first time I saw this gentle young woman in yellow delicately holding an open book in her right hand, I was smitten. I adored her soft, blushing cheeks, her full-figured physique, and her finely carved, gorgeously contoured features. But most of all, I loved the way she gazed at the book. She was enthralled, transported into a world of the imagination, a place that existed only in that book. Oh yes, I admired her great beauty, but I craved her peace and I coveted her ability to remove herself from this world. I needed to know her.

So, I researched madly. I studied every text, every article, every snatch of information that existed on that painting. I went to the National Gallery in Washington and spent hours in the Rococo gallery where she hung. I spoke with the experts, to the extent that they would share their time. I got to know Fragonard and that painting as well as I knew myself. Better. But all my research failed to answer the questions I cared about most: who she was, and why Fragonard had painted her.

So I made it up.

Yes, my much-discussed thesis was a fake, a phony, a sham. I'm proud to say I fooled the brightest minds in the business by knowing as much real information as anyone alive and by ever-so-carefully attributing my bogus information. I footnoted hundreds of sources and included reams of citations from interviews I had supposedly conducted—including critical ones with an expert "recently deceased" and therefore somewhat difficult for anyone to authenticate. Don't get me wrong, my thesis contained a great deal of valid information, but the "new information," the "facts" that meant the most to me and that revealed the whos, whys, and wherefores of this delicious painting, were entirely of my devising.

"This dissertation is so well-written," my advisor had said, "and contains such new and spicy information, I think you should take it to a commercial publisher. You could turn this into a mass market biography." He chuckled as he looked at me over his horn-rimmed half glasses. "Why just go for glory when you can go for money?"

I didn't go for either. I was not so dull-witted as to risk blowing my cover through such foolishness. The money was of no interest to me (my family had plenty), and I was not on a quest for glory. I had simply created a story I needed to tell myself, a story I came to adore and believe about how the young girl—Martine, I named her—was the artist's lover.

It was a happy coincidence that by doing so, I established my *bona fides* in the one community that mattered to me and gained entry into the curatorial world.

φ

"Columbia's a great choice, son," my father had said when I announced my college decision.

I smiled, pleased to have finally done something of which he approved.

"It'll be fine to have you here in town so you can intern at the firm." He slapped me on the back, nearly knocking me off my narrow feet. "Every investment bank needs bright young business majors."

I continued to smile but looked away from him. I wanted to maintain my silence and savor the blessing for as long as possible. But I finally spoke up.

"I'm not going to be a business major, Dad." The words came out very quietly, almost like a whisper; my voice was high and trembling.

"No? What then? Political science?" He laughed and slapped my back again. "God, Senator Mike Handley. Has a ring to it."

I shook my head.

"Don't tell me you're going to be an English major!" More laughter.

"Art history," I mumbled.

"Ha! That's a good one." Another slap, harder this time. His own voice was now pitched higher by just a few notes and his eyes betrayed a tiny apprehension that belied his jovial demeanor. "Real fag pursuit, huh?" More laughter. "Come on, what are you *really* going to major in?"

I didn't laugh with him, nor did I smile. "I'm going to be an art history major," I repeated.

It was his turn to be silent. But the silence didn't last long.

φ

After the conservator, the National Gallery's assistant curator, and I had completed a thorough examination of the painting, I directed that it be hung in the central gallery of the "Eighteenth Century French Fantasies" exhibition we were in the process of installing. Naturally, I had reserved a place of honor for the Fragonard; it was to be the visual and academic centerpiece around which the other works would revolve. The placement had been controversial, as some had argued that the two Watteaus in the show were more important, but, as curator of the exhibit, I prevailed.

φ

I visited the painting each evening when the museum closed its doors to the public. I walked through the empty, echoing marble corridors into the special exhibition galleries and stood before that young girl in yellow, my Martine, for hours at a time. I often spoke to her, maybe out loud, maybe not. I'm not sure. Then I did the unthinkable. I touched her. I ran my hands over her face, her sweet pale neck, her ruffled collar, and even her breast. I felt the *craquelure*, the *impasto*, and the smooth thin washes of background color.

Those moments with the young woman the world came to know, thanks to my thesis, as Martine Pelouse, were moments of perfect peace. She was in my museum and in my care. She was mine. When I allowed myself to think about the temporary nature of the exhibition, I grew despondent, and when those inevitable final days were upon me, my sadness changed to panic, even terror. I wondered how I would learn to live without her. That's when I knew for sure, though I suspect I may have known on some level from the very outset, that I would have to bring Martine home.

φ

I was twelve when I first saw her, on a prep school trip to Washington, D.C. The entire afternoon in question was designated for the National Gallery of Art, much to the dismay of my classmates.

"Why the hell do we have to do this art shit?"

That was a quote from the class president and an accurate encapsulation of the general attitude toward the scheduled adventure.

"Maybe we can lose the group and go back to Natural History…or just hit the streets for a while."

That was our elected vice president.

"I've heard there are nudie statues at the National Gallery," one wiry little boy contributed.

"Yeah?"

"Yeah. Big-titted babes right out in plain view. My brother told me he copped a feel when no one was looking."

"No lie?"

"No lie."

"Okay," said the president. "We'll give it a few minutes, but if the skin show's not all you say, I'm outa there."

And off we all went.

Of course, I did not share the views of the majority. I never had and, I suppose, never really will. But it didn't matter, as the other boys never asked my opinion. The fact is, I considered myself lucky when they ignored me entirely.

I was a short, fat boy whose best feature was a beautiful head of thick, shiny brown hair. Which I lost at the age of 25. I wore the same navy blue blazer and school tie as the other boys, but there the similarities ended. I had no interest in girls or sports or anything else that involved disrobing, in whole or in part, in front of other people. I was an average student who performed below average in class because of a painful shyness and uncontrollable stutter. I didn't care about enormous stuffed animals, mummies, skeletons or any of the other macho artifacts to be found in a natural history institution, nor did I care about copping feels.

But I loved art. Secretly, of course.

φ

At the National Gallery, we all trailed dutifully along behind a matronly docent in squeaky crepe-soled shoes who tried valiantly but in vain to maintain our attention. Feels were, in fact, copped by some of the boys as we walked through the huge airy sculpture corridors. Then leers, one-to-ten ratings, and manly laughter were exchanged as we passed paintings of fleshy women by the likes of Titian and Tintoretto.

I caught my first glimpse of Martine in a gallery where the docent spoke to us about Francois Drouais' "Group Portrait." While I had to acknowledge the craftsman like rendering of light and texture, I hated the picture. It portrayed a beautiful, sweet-faced mother, in the midst of her morning *toilette*, surrounded by her smiling husband and cloyingly contented little girl.

Families, I knew, were not like that, and I hated the artist who implied that this was real, this was natural, this was the way life was. For I too had a beautiful mother and a smiling father, but only at certain, carefully designated times. Mother was beautiful and father was smiling between the hours of six and midnight while they were entertaining or being entertained. During the rest of the day, Mother was drinking or hung over and Father was absent.

While the docent relentlessly parsed this sickening family and deconstructed their ritualistic activities, I allowed my eyes to wander around the walls of the gallery. I recognized the pastel colors and frou-frou style of the eighteenth century, but was unfamiliar—and unimpressed—with most of these works, until I saw Martine hanging quietly in the corner of the room.

I think it was the color that first grabbed me— that surprising splash of bright yellow amidst the faded pastels of the room. I wandered away from the group to get a closer look at Martine, although I did not yet know her by name. I was greatly impressed that she was not engaged in the inane games or parties of the subjects on the walls around her. Instead, she simply sat against a huge, soft pillow, reading a book.

Looking back, I believe that what ultimately lured me into her clutches was the fact that she had escaped and was living exactly where I wanted to live. She lived alone, in a peaceful mindscape that she herself had chosen. No one could bother her, no one could make fun of her. If her parents fought and yelled and threw things, she wouldn't hear. She was at perfect peace. It was not only written on her features but demonstrated in the way her left hand draped so easily, so limply, over the armrest.

I had, at that moment, what I have since heard Philippe de Montebello refer to as a "bolt out of the blue" experience. I fell instantly in love; I coveted her and her serenity, especially during the weeks and months immediately following my mother's death from an overdose of pills and alcohol, which occurred on the last day of my Washington field trip.

φ

I cannot claim that I intentionally engineered my career to arrive at a place where I could finally possess Martine. I've never been quite that clever or quite that directed. It was more of an evolution, and one that began even before Martine and I met.

The Metropolitan Museum had long been my refuge. It was where I sought quiet, beauty and solitude in a world filled with cacophony, nastiness, and constant judgments. I would walk there after school nearly every day to find an oasis between the taunts of my schoolmates, criticisms of my teachers, sulkiness or anger of my mother, and disappointment of my father.

The golden glow of Rembrandt soothed me, and the epic dramas he portrayed put my troubles into perspective. The gentle Madonnas of Raphael and Andrea del Sarto transported me to a sacred realm that had nothing to do with religion. The sunny impressionist landscapes suggested a beautiful world that existed somewhere outside of New York.

Not that it was all sunny. I didn't like the darkness and brutality of Daumier—too real. I hated the avant-garde chic of the abstract expressionists— too depressing. The African masks frightened me, and the Egyptian mummies reminded me of my own mortality. But in those days, I learned that I cared about art and that it the only world in which I could live. Thus I was able—no, compelled—to pursue my career despite the deep-cutting barbs of my father and the disdain of those who populated his universe.

φ

So it was that, over forty years after my first trip to the National Gallery, Martine came to inhabit the walls of my museum and, finally, my home.

I waited until the last day of the exhibition—the day before she was to have been crated up, nailed shut, and shipped back to Washington—before I made my move. I had shared a glass of champagne with my staff, in honor of our show's success, and sent them home. Then I took two bottles of champagne to the museum's night guards as a token of my gratitude for the extra responsibilities they had undertaken during the show's run.

I pulled the cork from one bottle, and it opened with a pop that echoed through the empty galleries like a gunshot. I filled two of those horrible plastic champagne flutes with sparkling liquid, and handed one to each guard.

"We're not supposed to drink on duty, Mr. Handley," one said with a grin that told me he was prepared to breach the rule if I insisted.

"But this is a special occasion, Mr. Fernandez. Please, it's on me." I held an empty glass in the air as if to toast. "Here's to the protective staff and a job well done."

"Cheers," the two men responded in unison. Each took a tentative sip.

"I'll be here in the galleries for a bit, if you gentlemen would like to sit down and enjoy your wine."

They looked at each other, then at me.

"Oh, go on. Before the bubbles fade."

"Thanks, Mr. Handley," the more senior guard said. "We'll be in our office if you need anything."

"I'm sure I'll be fine. And thank you, gentlemen, for all your hard work."

That was that.

φ

Miraculously, the theft was not discovered for two days. As curator, I was charged with dismantling the show, so I took advantage of the chaos created by the taking down, examining, and packing up of some thirty loaned works, to keep the staff sufficiently preoccupied and off-base that Martine's disappearance was not immediately noted.

During those forty-eight hours, and the surreal weeks that followed, she hung happily and peacefully in my home.

Of course, I took ordinary precautions, such as keeping the drapes closed and having new, more secure locks installed on my doors, but I did not hide Martine. I wanted her to live with me and share my life. I didn't roll her up and store her in a hole in a basement wall. I didn't wrap her in blankets and stash her in a closet. I did not wish to treat her as a dirty bit of contraband, so I hung her on my bedroom wall, just over the mantelpiece. Each evening after undressing, I would powder my body with talc so that I would smell sweet and fresh for her. I kept a tiny light shining on her throughout the night, and I lay in my bed and stared at her. She was finally mine.

Sometimes I would read to her on those languid summer nights; other times we would each read silently. Often, I simply gazed at her glorious countenance while she sat poring over her book. When I slept, I know she looked down at me; I could feel her eyes, filled with deep affection, piercing the haze of sleep and breaking through the fog of my existence.

During those days, I thought only of Martine. Each moment, even at work, was devoted to her. Once her disappearance was discovered, I actually enjoyed the intrusion of police and FBI agents and the endless meetings with my Director and representatives of the National Gallery because they kept my attention focused squarely on her.

I loved the secret she and I shared. After a lifetime of being the brunt of the joke, the object of ridicule, I was suddenly holding the proverbial cards. I was the one who had perpetrated the joke and had fooled them all. No one even thought to consider that Michael Handley, harmless old fogey of a curator, could be capable of such a thing.

No one except those damnable guards. Of course, they were my undoing.

Not that this came as a big surprise to me. On some level, I knew from the very start that Martine, in her corporeal form, would not be mine forever. And I knew that I would pay dearly for the abduction. I also knew it would be worth it.

φ

My cell was bleak, as one might expect. A commode in the corner, a small table, a narrow cot. Walls of concrete block. A window too high to look through, adorned, of course, with the requisite iron bars.

Life there was simpler than I'd ever found it. I arose when told to, ate meals when served, and took a bit of exercise—a slow walk, usually—when the opportunity was offered. Some of my time was devoted to folding papers for the state and inserting them in envelopes, an activity I found surprisingly soothing. No one expected anything of me, so I never failed to meet expectations.

When my block mates sat at the end of the corridor and watched television, I was generally granted permission to read the single book I had brought with me, a small catalogue of works in the National Gallery of Art. Designed for tourists, the book was woefully lacking in useful information, but the reproductions were lovely, so I felt privileged to spend time, even there, with my Martine.

φ

I live in Washington now, and quite comfortably, thanks to a generous inheritance from my father. There is a delicious irony, I think, in the notion that this man, who harbored such hostility toward the visual arts, now, from the grave, provides me with the means to live near and spend time with my Martine.

And that I do, for she continues to dominate my still-very-ordered existence. I arrive at the National Gallery when it opens each day at ten in the morning, eleven on Sundays, and I sit with Martine until closing time at five. Our blessings are abundant, but our pleasures quite simple. We continue to read, aloud or silently, and to enjoy the warmth of each others' presence. I sometimes pen sonnets for her, or the occasional haiku, which I recite standing before her. The Gallery's protective staff keeps a watchful eye on us, knowing our history, but they generally leave us alone.

While I miss her desperately at night, and on Christmas and New Year's Day when the Gallery locks its doors, I cherish the time we do have together. And I bear my loneliness and celibacy bravely in the hope that one day I will see her inhabit, once and for all, the empty gilded frame that awaits her above the mantelpiece in my Georgetown home.

φφφ

Judy Pomeranz is a freelance writer, lecturer and art critic. Her articles have appeared in a wide range of newspapers and magazines and her short stories and essays have been published in literary journals including *Santa Barbara Review, Potomac Review, Crescent Review, Fodderwing,* and *MassAve Review,* as well as in the anthologies, *Great Writers, Great Stories* and *Chesapeake Crimes II.* Her novella, *On the Far Edge of Love,* is currently being serialized in *élan* magazine which also serialized her earlier novellas, *Lies Beneath the Surface* and *Elegy.*

Judy holds an M.A. in writing from Johns Hopkins University, teaches writing at Georgetown University, and has won prizes and recognition in fiction contests sponsored by The National Press Club, the DC Bar, and *élan* magazine.

THE KOSHER PICKLE MURDER
by Ellen Rawlings

Saul Golden came to the US from Russia in 1896. With him he brought Sarah, his wife, and the two children they had then. Occasionally through the years, Joan Levy, his first-born granddaughter, asked him why he'd left his village. He always shook his head and said it wasn't worth talking about.

So she was surprised when one day he brought up the subject. They were sitting in his large kitchen in South Philadelphia at the time. Joan was enjoying its old-fashioned, homey furnishings, so different from her parents' slick new appliances, and the rich smell of the chicken soup simmering in a large white pot at the back of the stove. Before her grandfather was his usual glass of tea. In the saucer was a sugar cube he sucked the tea through. "I've been thinking," he said. "Do you know how lucky you are to be in this country?"

"Sure I do." Her pretty face was as intent as his.

"You couldn't know the way I do. The Old Country wasn't so lucky for our people." He paused. "You want to hear why I left?" He spoke in Yiddish. The Russian language was practically unknown to him, as was English.

Ah, at last. She leaned closer across the linoleum-covered table. "Tell me."

"It was because of a kosher pickle."

"*Zaida*! Stop teasing."

Her grandfather gave her a look that told her she should keep her mouth shut and listen. She closed her lips obediently. All the family deferred to him: his wife, his children, and his grandchildren. Saul Golden was the patriarch; thus he was to be obeyed.

Joan's grandfather was a large man in every sense of the word. He was over six feet, a great height back then, with a big frame, and hands that could life the heaviest burden seemingly without strain. His emotions were large, too. If he laughed, he did it heartily. The same went for crying. And nobody ever suggested, or even considered, that his weeping was unmanly.

"Okay, it went like this. One day after *schul*, Joshua, one of the old rabbi's sons, came to me and asked if I'd be willing to bring his father maybe two pickles. He said I had the best pickles in the whole *shtetl* and it would make his father very happy.

"Of course, I said yes. You know how to prepare them?" he interrupted his story to ask Joan. She shook her head no. "Vinegar and water," he said. "to make up a gallon of liquid, kosher salt, pickling spices, celery tops, and garlic. Plus my secret ingredient: four small dried red peppers, the hottest ones you can find. Then you leave it until the cucumbers are still firm but not hard."

Her mouth watered. "Do you have any now?"

"No, not now. Listen. This guy Mordechai, a real drunk and a wife beater, pushed his way between us and said he could give the Rabbi better. He said his pickles were the best to be had in the *shtetl*, maybe in the whole country . . . and he could prove it.

"I started to turn my back on the braggart, but stopped when Joshua asked him what he had in mind. He said by having a contest: that we should both bring pickles and let the men of the village taste and decide. He looked directly at me then and asked me if I was afraid to agree.

"Naturally, I accepted the challenge."

"Oh, naturally," she said. She knew her grandfather.

"Two weeks later," he went on, "when my pickles were at their prime, we met outside the *schul*, with our samples in sacks. I pulled out a beautiful pickle, just right, light green, not mushy inside but cured all the way through, smelling of garlic, and dripping juice. And what did that *momser* take out? A picked green tomato, not a pickle at all!"

As he spoke, her grandfather's face reddened. He banged his huge first on the table, making the spoons jump. Obviously, even after all those years, he was still angry. "You can understand I objected."

"Yes, indeed," she said, knowing that was all that was expected of her.

"So, anyway, the judges didn't listen; they tasted my pickles and his tomatoes. And you know what they decided, the cowards? That mine was the best pickle and Mordechai's the best pickled tomato. I didn't even bother to complain anymore. I snatched the remaining piece of pickle out of the hands of the rabbi's son, dropped it in the dirt, and left."

"And that is why you came to the United States?" she asked, looking skeptical. It didn't seem like much of a reason to her.

He looked at her impatiently. "Not exactly. The murder and the pig had the most to do with it." He pushed back his chair and stood. "I need more tea."

Joan was amazed when he mentioned a murder; no one in the family had ever hinted of such a thing. Nor had anyone, as far as she could remember, referred to an incident involving a pig.

To tell the truth, she was almost as amazed that he got the tea himself. As long as she could recall, he yelled for her grandmother, no matter what she was doing, to come in the kitchen and serve him.

He sat down and took a sip of the hot tea that would have scalded the lining off the inside of Joan's mouth. "Where was I? Yes, the next day someone banged at the door. I recognized him; it was one of the Russians' policemen. I admit it: my heart gave a thump. When they showed up, there was always trouble for us."

He looked at the clock on the wall and gulped down the rest of his tea. "It's time for me to go to *schul*."

"Wait," she said. "Who was murdered?"

"Mordechai, of course."

"And the authorities thought you did it? You've got to tell me what happened next."

"When I come back, I'll finish." He stood, adjusted his rumpled gray suit, pushed down a black hat over his *yarmulkah,* and left the room.

She should have known he wouldn't stay home from *schul.* The other men in her grandfather's synagogue would be waiting for him to help make up a *minion,* the ten men necessary for a service to be held. With nothing else to keep her occupied, she decided to go for a walk.

She was familiar with the neighborhood, having been taken to visit her grandparents from the time she was little, so she hardly noticed the three-story brownstone houses that lined both sides of the street, the trolley tracks that ran down its center, or the lack of even a wren because there weren't any trees. There wasn't any shade, either. She could feel herself perspiring in the close July air.

What Joan was aware of were the distant sound of a train whistle and the group of colorfully dressed gypsies who rented part of one of the brownstones at the other end of the block. She hoped they'd be out of sight before her grandfather returned. He didn't like them, and when one of them came near his property, he'd yell, "Get the hell, get out of here" in his convoluted English.

He definitely had a temper, but could he have committed murder?

Her grandfather returned about an hour later and, after more tea, picked up where he'd left off in his story. "The policeman told me Mordechai had been found dead from a poisoned pickle. I knew right away where that was going. I asked how he could be sure it was poison. He told me the proof was the description given by the victim's wife of the way Mordechai suffered while he was dying.

"I asked him how anyone in our *shtetl* would get poison. This policeman, he sneered at me. 'As though you don't know. Everyone has it—you have it—to kill the rats and the bedbugs.' There was a pause while I looked at him. 'What's worse, though, is the pig.'

"'The pig?'

"'In back of this Mordechai's house is the farm of the Kravchuks. Their prize sow died that same night. The owner said it was poisoned. I know how you people are about pigs.'

"'You think the death of a pig is worse?' I said, ignoring his comment about our religious taboo against pork.

"He said, 'What's another dead *Zhyd?*'"

Her grandfather shook his head. "That's when I started to think seriously about emigrating. You want some fruit?"

He was always trying to feed her. She guessed it was an expression of Eastern European hospitality that he shared with others, both Jew and gentile, from that region. "No, just the story."

"Okay. The man asked me if I wanted to save time and confess. He said he'd heard about the contest and figured that I was seeking revenge. I made myself laugh, though it was no laughing matter. He'd have been just as happy to see me hang as anyone else in the *shtetl*. I said, 'Over a pickle? You've got the wrong person, Sir. Now, if it was money...'

"I knew how they thought about us, and I used it. He accepted what I said, gave me a slap on the back, and left. I drank some Sabbath wine, to take the taste of that 'Sir' out of my mouth.

"Sarah had stayed out of sight while the policeman was there. She came into the room when he left. She said, 'My God, Saul, I heard what the gentile said. Who could have done such a thing?'

"I told her I didn't know, but that I had a good idea who would be punished for it—me!"

"'You? That's ridiculous.'

"'You know it, I know it, and the murderer knows it, but the police don't. What's more, they don't care.'

"She said, 'Then we need to find out who it really was. How about Yenkel? He has a bad temper and he hates Mordechai.' I shook my head no. I said, he'd never use poison. A hammer is a possibility, but not poison.

"'Then, Abraham, maybe. Remember, he wanted to marry Leah and was very upset when her father chose Mordechai instead?'

"'I don't think so. He can't even slap a gnat that's sitting on his arm.'

"She stood, tied her kerchief around her hair, and walked to the door. I said, 'Where are you going?'

"'To visit poor Leah.'

"I wasn't convinced she should; but I could tell from the way she said it, I wouldn't be able to change her mind, so I didn't bother to try."

Joan didn't want to interrupt him, but she couldn't help herself. "*Bubba?*" Her grandmother was perhaps four foot eight, round as a dumpling, sweet, and soft-spoken. She was not assertive.

He nodded and said, "You don't know her. She can be stubborn. Anyway, she came back maybe an hour later and told me that Leah killed her husband. I asked her how she could know that.

"Sarah's hands twisted in her apron over what she was going to tell me. 'He beat her. One of her eyes was swollen shut and she had a front tooth missing.'

"'He's done that before. How is that proof?'

"Sarah said, 'I will find a way to prove it. I am sorry for Leah, but if I don't you will always be suspected of killing him, if the authorities don't hang you first.'

"I said of course she should do it. Should I give up my life because of that no-good Mordechai?

"That night Sarah went again to visit the widow. Naturally, I expected to go with her, but she said no, that I would grow impatient and burst into Leah's house, which would ruin everything. She said one of the other men in the village would go with her. I didn't like that, either, but she said she would leave me if I didn't stay home." He sighed. "I didn't really believe her, but, on the other hand, why take a chance? When your grandmother makes up her mind, the Angel of Death himself couldn't convince her to change it.

"Okay, when she came back maybe an hour later, I was asleep. She woke me and said not to worry. Leah had confessed.

"'Why would she do that?' I asked her. 'How did you get her to confess?'

"She said I should remember that she'd known Leah from the time she was little, so she was aware how superstitious she was, that she tied everything with red ribbons to keep away this or that, and she always spat *ptui, ptui* to ward off the evil eye.

"'So?' I asked Sarah. 'What are you telling me?'

"She said, 'I went into her house, leaving Josele outside.'

"'Josele? Which one? I can think of at least three of that name.'

"'Mordechai's brother.'

"'Ah.'

"'It was dark, with only one candle lit. The smell of the cows in their stalls in the next room was very strong. Leah was sitting in a chair. I could hardly see her, so I moved the candle closer. She was slumped over. At first I thought she was dead, but then I heard her cough. I said, *It's Sarah. I've come back again.* She repeated my name, as though otherwise she might forget it.

"'I knelt beside her and took her hand. It was so cold. I said, *Leah, you have to tell me what really happened to Mordechai.*

"She said, *What happened? Why ask me? All I know is he ate a big bite of pickle. Then he grabbed his stomach, fell down, and vomited. He had convulsions and he died. The police say he was murdered.*

"'Where did he get the pickle?

"'She shrugged.

"'You can't say who killed him?

"'She tried to look surprised, but she wasn't a good actress. She said, *Me? Of course I can't.*

"'I was sure she was guilty, but, also, I was sure she wouldn't confess to me. I went to the door and opened it, my hand over my nose so she'd believe I needed air because of the cows. Josele was still there.

He was dressed up in a sheet so Leah would think it was Mordechai's ghost. I waved Josele inside. I'd already told him what I thought he should say to her and how he should act. He pronounced her name the way Mordechai would—only weaker like someone who wasn't alive any more.

"'She screamed. Josele waited for her to stop, and then he said to Leah that she had to tell the truth about the murder; otherwise he wouldn't be able to rest and he'd have to stay with her and torment her forever. She started to moan, rocking back and forth like a person in pain. He kept whispering, *Confess. Confess.*

"'Finally she did. She said she couldn't stand being beaten anymore, so she put rat poison in one of his pickles.'

"Not a tomato?" I asked.

"She shook her head. 'A pickle. Leah said it was so full of garlic and spices, he didn't taste the poison. A little bit later, he died. I would have felt sorry for her, because Mordechai was such a terrible man, but I couldn't. I could see she didn't care if you were accursed of the murder.'

"'And the pig?' I asked.

"'For a moment your *bubba* looked as though she didn't know what I was talking about. Then she remembered. She said that Leah threw the rest of the pickle onto the farmer's property and, though she hadn't intended to kill him, she imagined the pig ate it.

"I said, 'She'll be arrested today, for killing the pig.'

"Sarah looked upset. I said, 'Don't worry. Among the *shtetl* families, we should be able to scrape together enough money to pay for the pig and bribe the policeman. And give Mordechai a proper burial, too, though he doesn't deserve it. Nothing will happen to Leah, except that she'll be shunned. Who's going to be friendly with a husband killer?'"

He said back in his chair and looked at his American granddaughter. "That's the story."

Joan asked, "Did your predictions come true?"

He shrugged. "Of course. Don't I know what I'm talking about?" It sounded like a question, but it wasn't. Her grandfather was not afflicted with self-doubt.

"And what happened after that?" she asked him.

"Nothing special. I added to my savings for the next two years till we could afford the passage to the United States. Then we left."

Joan and her grandfather had been sitting a long time. She pushed away her empty tea glass, stood, and stretched. She said, "I'm glad you told me that story. I always wondered."

"Okay, now you don't need to."

"If you don't mind," she said, leaning over to touch his nearer hand. "I want to believe you saved the family from the barbarian with a kosher pickle. I don't know why, but that appeals to me."

For the first time since he began his tale, he smiled. "That's all right with me. Think what you want; it's your story now, too. You want me to get you a pickle? I have some that are perfect."

φφφ

Ellen Rawlings has written both mysteries and regency romances. *The Murder Lover* and *Deadly Harvest*, from Fawcett, feature freelance Columbia, Maryland journalist Rachel Crowne.

SECOND WIFE ONCE REMOVED
by Audrey Sherins

I pushed open the front door and took a few steps on my way to pick up the morning paper when I came face to face with a man I didn't know. When I saw the trash collection truck at the bottom of my driveway I realized that the man before me belonged to it.

"What's the matter?" I asked. "Did I forget to recycle something again?"

"Ma'am, please call the police," the man said in a calm voice.

"You're going to report me to the recycling police?" I joked. "I promise I'll never do it again, just don't turn me in." I put my hands up in a surrender motion.

"Please, lady," he said very seriously. "Call the police."

"What is it? What's wrong? Has there been an accident?"

He started to walk back down the driveway to the truck and I followed him. As I moved closer to the bottom a slight breeze, in the already humid air, brought the fetid odor of decay to my nostrils. Ah, summertime in the D.C. suburbs, I thought. The man's partner was standing beside a large, green, plastic trash bag that was clearly full.

"Is this yours?" the second man asked pointing to the plastic bag.

"No, I always put my trash in this wheeled container," I said pointing to it. "Someone must have left the bag here." I walked toward the garbage bag.

"I wouldn't touch that if I were you," said the first man.

"Why not?"

"Because there's a body inside it."

I looked. It was Carla, my ex-husband's soon-to-be ex, but I guessed she was that already considering her present condition. Well, at least it would save him the cost of an untidy divorce. What was she doing here, I wondered, messing up my driveway the way she had messed up my whole life?

The police came, along with an ambulance that took the body away, and the entire neighborhood lined up to gawk at the spectacle. Yellow police tape was strung among my trees and everyone was looking at me as if I were Public Enemy Number One. The only thing missing was a chalk outline of the body.

I went inside and busied myself making coffee for the police and finally sat down with the detectives who wanted to question me.

"Did you know the deceased?"

"You could say that," I told them.

"How's that?" This from the good-looking detective who had a dimple in his chin à la Sean Connery.

"She's my ex-husband's current wife." No need to tell them that he was in the process of dumping her. Not many people knew this and technically I had been sworn to secrecy.

I remembered the first time I had seen Carla. She was hired to work in the offices of our family drug company, the one that Howie and I had started and built from scratch.

She teetered in on her spike heels, all five feet of her, and turned the head of everyone working there. People employed in other parts of the building made excuses to come to the office area just to catch a glimpse of her. She was a stunner. Wavy auburn hair framed a glowing face and large amber eyes sized up everybody and everything around, while her pouty lips seemed to puzzle over the details. She oozed sex appeal and had she been taller she might have made it as a model or a showgirl, but her voice would have closed the door to Hollywood with the utterance of just one syllable. It was a high-pitched singsong, both nasal and grating, like an untuned guitar string being plucked over and over again. If I listened to her for too long I wanted to cover my ears to shut out the rasping. From the beginning Carla, with dollar signs flashing in her eyes, had made Howie her pet project.

"How long has Carla been married to your ex-husband?"

"It's been two years. She came to work for our company about a year before that."

"Company?"

"Yes, Howie and I own Howel Drugs. We started it and built it from the ground up. We even put our names together to name it. You know 'How' from Howard and 'el' from the end of my name, Rachel."

Howie had been a chemistry major in college, when we met, and after we married I worked to support us and put him through pharmacy school. We managed to scrape together enough money to open a small drug store in a suburban neighborhood and went on to build it into a chain of thirty-seven stores in three states. Not too bad for a couple of small town kids. We both worked hard to build the business and could hardly believe our success as the years went by, but even though all was going well in the business side of our lives, Howie had trouble dealing as mid-life approached. He bought himself a red Ferrari and other expensive toys that conveyed a sense of youth, but none of them did the trick for more than a few months. He hired a personal trainer, shopped for clothes at trendy, expensive stores, and talked of building a huge new house, in spite of the fact that the two of us were already rattling around in our present home. I should have seen it coming.

Although she had a Frederick's of Hollywood catalogue body Carla was a bright girl with all the right moves. The sound of ka-ching was in the air as she sized up our business. She could see how vulnerable Howie was and slowly moved into his life as she pressed me out of it, with the ease of squeezing toothpaste out of a tube. Before long she became Mrs. Trophy Wife and I became the ex. The whole thing turned my ego into the size of a pea. I retained one of the best divorce lawyers in the country and ended up with half the business and a lot more, but even though I wasn't hurting for money my pride had been stomped on.

"When was the last time you saw Carla?" The older, gruffer police detective asked, breaking into my reverie.

"It was Monday morning."

"You seem pretty sure."

"I am. I went to pick up Truffles at their house."

"Truffles? Your daughter?"

"No, our dog. Here she comes now."

Hearing her name Truffles walked into the kitchen, her tail wagging. She stretched her front paws like a gymnast warming up and yawned, still groggy from her morning nap, but eager to meet and befriend the strangers in her home. Bichon frisees are not watchdog material; they're just too loving. The worst they can do is lick you to death. Truffles began her own investigation of the men sitting in her kitchen by sniffing their shoes and trouser bottoms, but I swiftly sent her outside just in case this annoyed them.

"We have joint custody of Truffles," I told the two men. "Howie and Carla had her over the weekend and I picked her up and brought her home on Monday. That was the last time I saw Carla." Howie never really cared that much about Truffles. We had no children, but he knew how much I adored the dog and insisted on joint custody to get back at me in some petty way for getting half of the business. I went along with the shared arrangement, but always thought that Truffles was much happier to be back with me each time she returned.

"Did you have words with Carla the last time you saw her? Did you argue?"

"No."

"How did you get along?" This from the cute detective.

"Okay I guess. We didn't spend a lot of time on chit chat. Howie used to have her call and tell me what to do with Truffles. 'Howie says Truffles needs to have her nails clipped,' or 'Howie says the groomer didn't do a good job last time.' I spoke in the high-pitched whiny voice Carla used, but couldn't carry off the twang. "She was our go-between, our conduit," I explained. "That's all."

What I didn't tell the detectives was that the last time Carla called to tell me "Howie says" I let her have it. Told her if Howie had anything to say he could tell me directly. Then I yelled at her and accused her of mistreating Truffles, something I had suspected for a long time. I really read her the riot act. Inside of every red-blooded woman there is an inner bitch waiting to erupt. At that point I had had it with Carla up to the top, and I guess my personal Vesuvius spewed forth. For all I knew she was making it all up just to irritate me, and Howie never asked her to tell me anything.

"Do you think your ex-husband killed Carla?"

I laughed. "Howie? I doubt it."

"Do you know if she had any enemies?"

"I'm not really sure, but a conniver like her must have collected a few along the way."

The police searched my house and yard, with my permission, of course—I had nothing to hide—and then they left. The yellow tape in front of the house remained, however, flapping whenever a rare breeze rippled it. Silently it called to all around, "here is crime, here is death, here is murder" in the way old pirate maps stated, "here be dragons." Unfortunately that "here" just happened to be my front yard, and I wondered why.

After our divorce my friends introduced me to a succession of eligible men in whom I had little interest. On my own I met Blake Allcott, a decent, caring, and kind man who was one of the top criminal lawyers on the east coast. Blake was a bulldog in the courtroom, but with me he was the gentlest soul I had ever met, and the fact that he was drop dead gorgeous didn't hurt. If Howie could walk around with a sex goddess on his arm I could have Mr. Handsome on mine, and it certainly took my ex-husband back when he saw Blake and me together for the first time.

I called Blake soon after the police left and told him what had gone on. Unlike the homicide detectives he was courteous enough not to ask me if I had killed Carla.

"Did the police interview you?" Blake asked.

"Yes, we talked forever about Carla and me and Howie too. They asked the same questions over and over, I guess trying to catch me in a lie, but they seemed satisfied and left without carting me off in handcuffs. They also searched my house and yard, but found nothing because there was nothing to find. Except for Carla's body, of course."

"Did you tell them about the car that almost ran over you and Truffles?" Blake asked.

"No, it didn't occur to me." Several weeks before, I had been out walking Truffles one night when a car, with headlights off, sped toward us and would have hit us if I hadn't heard it at the last minute and, clutching Truffles, slid down a steep incline.

Fortunately we escaped with only cuts and bruises.

"At any rate, if they want to talk to you again call me first. I want to be there."

"Should I do anything?" I asked.

"No, just sit tight. I'll try to look into what's going on and I'll either call you or see you later tonight if that's okay with you."

"Sure," I answered, eagerly looking forward to an evening with Blake to help blot out the harsh realities of the day. And what a day it had been, waking up to find a dead body stashed at the bottom of my driveway, and that coming soon after the near hit-and-run experience that could have sent Truffles and me into never-never land.

Dear Blake. Just talking to him had taken away some of the tension. He was so sweet to offer to snoop around and find out what the police knew, and to insist that I not talk to them again unless he was present. The man was such a love, so supportive, but I wondered what he might think if he knew about the phone call I made and what I had done. Would he be loyal and stick by me or would he dump me in a New York minute? Maybe, just maybe, he liked bad girls. It could be a turn on, exciting and sexy. Who could say? Of course then I'd have to tell him the whole story.

A few days after our almost hit-and-run experience I was taking Truffles to Howie and Carla for their required weekend with her. It was an unexpectedly nice summer day in the Washington suburbs, with bright sunshine but low humidity, so I decided to walk the half-mile or so. Truffles was happy to be outside and stopped to sniff every bush and tree where scores of dogs had gone before her. I took a short cut through a pathway adjacent to Howie's new house, rather than walk all the way around the block, and as we moved along the path I could hear Carla talking. She was probably sitting out by the pool and talking on her cell phone. Because of an eight-foot tall fence that surrounded the property and made a fortress of it, Carla could not see us, so I decided to listen in. Actually, I would have needed earplugs not to hear her for she started shouting loudly.

"What, you missed her? How could you? She's such an easy target waddling along with that stupid dog, and you missed her?"

Was she talking about what I thought she was talking about?

"You're going to have to do it right the next time, and no you can't do Howie first. I told you, if we knock her off first Howie will get her half of the business, and that means I'll get it all when he goes. That's the way their divorce settlement was worked out." She sounded as if she were talking to a young child who had misbehaved by running into the street and needed an explanation of the consequences. "Of course, I love you Joey, but you've got to kill her and then him so that we can be together with all of that money."

Joey who, I wondered? Carla talked on for a few minutes, but it was mostly yeses and noes on her end until she finally hung up. I backtracked and took the long way around the block to Carla's house. It was hard to face her and harder still to hand over my beloved Truffles to her, but I had to play the game and act as if I knew nothing. Carla hardly noticed me when she came to the door, and that was fine with me because I was sure I was still shaking from the realization that I was a marked woman. I felt guilty handing Truffles over to Carla, but knew I had to keep up the act.

I raced home, peeking over my shoulder the entire time and not crossing a street if there was a car within ten blocks. I didn't know what to do. There weren't a lot of options as far as I was concerned. I had seen Carla in action when she went after Howie and knew she had the single-minded determination of a spawning salmon swimming upstream. It was clear that Carla would kill for money even if she had to do it herself. I suppose I could have gone to the police, but I didn't have any real proof against Carla and if they questioned her she would be tipped off that I knew. As far as I was concerned, it had become the law of the jungle—kill or be killed.

I phoned my cousin, Stacy, my only living relative, who also had a lot to lose in this situation. She was my sole beneficiary. Stacy and I had grown up together and were as tight as ticks, and when I told her my situation she was in complete agreement with my decision.

"I told you Rach, that woman would be nothing but trouble, even after the divorce."

"I know, I know," I said. We had had this discussion before.

"You should have called the police when that car tried to hit you."

"I know," I said, getting a little irritated with her second-guessing, "but I didn't."

"Does Matt still keep in touch with his college roommate?" I asked, getting straight to the point.

"Gordon? Oh yeah. Of course!" She understood why I asked.

Stacy's husband, Matthew, had become friendly with a man whose family had mob connections. Gordon, Matt's friend, was a respectable lawyer and businessman, but knew the right people to get the job done when something outside the law was called for.

"I'll ask Matt to call Gordon and see what can be done," Stacy told me before she hung up.

A few nights later Stacy called with news that the contact had been made. The cost was less than I had expected it to be, (was a life worth so little?), and it would be done quickly. "I'm starting to feel a little squeamish about all this Stacy," I told her. "I'm not really a killer."

"Look Rachel, it's the only way, and it's not as if you have to do it yourself. Anyway it's all set now, so just look out for yourself, and make sure that you don't go for anymore nighttime walks with Truffles."

"Don't worry. I'm not even going to walk Truffles for a while." As an after-thought I asked, "You told him to make it look like an accident didn't you?"

Stacy reassured me and left me with words of encouragement. "You're doing the right thing Rachel."

Now, it appeared that the deed had been done, but why had Carla's body been dropped in front of my house. Was this some sort of blackmail attempt by the hit man? Maybe I should have given him more money. The amount asked for didn't seem like a lot, but I didn't even know who he was. I wondered if he knew me. I should have trusted my instincts and called off the whole thing when I had second thoughts, I told myself.

The doorbell rang and I ran to answer it expecting Blake to be at the door, but it wasn't Blake.

"Howie?"

"Hi, Rachel. Can I come in?"

"Well, yes, sure," I stammered.

Howie came in and we sat down in the family room. "I'm sorry about Carla," I told him.

"Don't be," he said. "She was a terrible woman."

I nodded. We both sat in silence for a few minutes and then Howie started to cry.

"Howie, what's wrong?"

"Rachel, I'm sorry."

"You mean the divorce? I'm over it Howie, in fact I'm having a great life."

"No." He looked at me very seriously. "Rachel, I put Carla's body at the bottom of your driveway."

"You killed her?"

"No, No I swear I didn't kill her. I came back to the house late last night, just to pick up a few things I had left behind. Did you hear I was leaving Carla?"

"I heard."

"Well, I found her lying on the floor in the kitchen. I checked for a pulse, for a breath, but she was dead. I didn't know what to do and I panicked. I figured the police would find out that I was leaving her and think that I killed her. Then I remembered that it was Thursday night and your trash was always collected on Friday morning. It seemed such a simple way to get rid of her, so I stuffed her body inside an extra large trash bag and left it at the bottom of your driveway. I was scared and it made sense at the time."

"Howie, you idiot. I can't believe you did this to me."

"I'm sorry Rachel. I wasn't trying to implicate you, I just wasn't thinking."

At least I didn't have to worry about a hit man blackmailing me anymore.

I never saw Blake that night. He had to go out of town on business, and I slept very little, tossing and turning in bed until dawn. Nightmares about Carla kept waking me. In one she was coming after me in a speeding car and there was no place to hide to get away from her, and in another, I was standing over her with a bloody knife in my hand. Guilt was leaking out of all my pores and I was starting to feel very jumpy. I just hoped the police wouldn't return to question me again.

Blake called a few days later when he returned. "Rachel, I just spoke to my friend in Baltimore."

"Baltimore?"

"Yes, the medical examiner released the autopsy report on Carla."

"Oh." I held my breath.

"It seems she died of natural causes."

"She did?" Boy, Gordon's guy was good. I had asked for an accident, but this was even better.

"Carla had a brain aneurysm that ruptured. She died instantly."

I wondered how he had done that. Must be tricks of the trade, I thought.

"Of course, the police still have the mystery of her body being in the trash bag. She couldn't have conveniently fallen into it when she died and then rolled to your driveway, but I'm sure the police will figure it out in time."

"Right." Poor Howie would eventually have to fess up to his involvement.

Once more we made plans to see each other.

I tried to call Stacy again. I had been trying to reach her ever since Carla's body had been found, but she never answered the phone. I had left a flood of messages on her answering machine, carefully ignoring any mention of Carla's death, and ended up leaving one more.

I didn't hear from Stacy for another day and when she did call she sounded terribly distressed.

"Oh, Rachel, I'm so sorry."

"Stacy, where have you been? I've been calling and calling."

"I know, I just heard your messages on my answering machine. We had to go away. Matt's mother was on some small island in the Caribbean with a friend, and she fell and broke her ankle. They couldn't do much with her there so we had to fly down and bring her to Florida for treatment. We just got back.

"Is she okay?" I asked.

"Yeah, sure, she's fine, but I'm worried about you and I'm afraid I have other bad news."

"Oh no. What?"

"Well, you know Matt's friend Gordon's friend?"

"Uh huh."

"He was driving to Maryland to do that job you asked him to do and it seems he lost control of his car on some back road. It flipped over and tumbled down a steep ravine. He died in the crash, but the car wasn't found until yesterday. Matt just spoke to Gordon who said not to worry.

"Oh my god," I said, slowly understanding the meaning of what she said and all that it implied.

"Don't worry Rachel, it's okay. Gordon said to tell you he'd get someone else on the job right away."

"It's okay," I murmured. "They already picked up the trash."

φφφ

Audrey Sherins is a founding member of Sisters in Crime's Chesapeake Chapter. In addition to her interest in mystery fiction, she has co-authored two non-fictions books: *How To Embarrass Your Kids Without Even Trying* and *The Joy of Grandparenting*. She has also contributed to a restaurant review column in *The Washington Post* and is currently writing a mystery novel.

THROUGH THE ROOF
by Verna Suit

Detective Sonny Erickson's brow furrowed as he contemplated the computer screen in front of him. A minute ago he'd been scrolling through the database of open cases. But apparently he'd done something he shouldn't have, because the display had suddenly changed to the department shift roster. To recover his place, he'd wildly clicked on anything that might get him back to where he'd been. Now he was hopelessly lost.

"Paper used to be so easy," he grumbled to his lieutenant, who was approaching. "I don't know why we have to do everything on the damn computer now. I just wasted an hour trying to find a witness name I could have gotten in thirty seconds from the file cabinet. And I still don't have the damn name."

"Well, forget about your name, we got a body. Check it out." Before Sonny left the office, the lieutenant explained that a dead body had been found in the debris after a natural gas explosion. "A private home, it was on the TV news last night. Arson squad got called in because circumstances looked suspicious. We got called because of the body."

In his unmarked police car, Sonny wound through the streets of a 25-year-old subdivision until he came to a knot of official vehicles. He stopped in front of what had once been a large, brick-facade residence on a street that was lined with the house's close cousins. The destroyed dwelling left a gap like a missing tooth. Men in boots and jumpsuits combed through the charred rubble, while news cameras filmed the explosion's aftermath.

Sonny buttonholed a sergeant from the arson squad to get an update. "Looks like somebody planned it, all right," said the sergeant. "Used the old gas-and-candle trick. Lit a candle in the living room, then turned on the gas stove and blew out the pilot light. By the time the gas reached the candle, enough had built up to blow the house sky high. Guy who died was the owner, Harry Cooper."

"Sure it wasn't an accident? Or a suicide?"

"If it was a suicide, it was a hell of a way to do it. He risked taking the rest of the neighborhood out with him. Plus if he wanted to make sure it was going to be fatal, he should have stayed downstairs where the main explosion was going to blow. But it doesn't look like he did that. Looks to me like he was upstairs in bed. The explosion did kill him, but only because it sent him clear through the roof. He broke his neck when he came down. And no, I don't think it was an accident, because there are signs somebody set it up—which is why we called you guys. It's not just arson anymore. Now it's murder."

The sergeant ticked off the evidence: the remnants of a candle, all four knobs of the gas stove turned to high, and signs of a break-in at a rear basement window. "The broken glass fell in instead of out, which is the direction it would have gone in an explosion"

Sonny surveyed the house's depressing remains, which still reeked of smoke and burned, wet wood. Then he noticed the dump truck parked at the curb directly in front of the lot. "You letting stuff be hauled away already?"

The sergeant followed Sonny's glance. "No, nobody ordered the truck. That was here when the explosion happened. Belongs to the roofers. Guy was in the process of getting a new roof." He added wryly, "Which is why he went through it so easy. I understand it was down to just rafters and plastic tarp." He walked over, picked up a muddied and water-stained sign that had been posted in the front yard, and held it up for Sonny to see. It read, "Roof by Redfield." Sonny jotted down the roofer's phone number.

Next he began talking with neighbors, who had finally been allowed back in their homes after being evacuated for safety. A short, gray-haired woman who lived across the street—Mrs. Meyers— was far from intimidated by the tall, bulky detective, and even seemed anxious to talk. "I hear I'm lucky to still be around," she said as she fixed him a glass of iced tea and settled him onto her living room couch. "Is it true the police think the explosion was set on purpose? Do you think somebody actually meant to kill Harry?"

News traveled fast. "It's a possibility we're looking into. Just in case it's true, can you think of anyone who might have wanted Harry Cooper dead?"

"Well, you could start with everybody in the neighborhood!" She gave a delighted chuckle, then leaned forward conspiratorially. "I don't mean that, of course. It's just that Harry wasn't an easy person to get along with. Nobody around here is going to miss him much."

"Anybody in particular not going to miss him?"

She rolled her eyes as if shocked at such a question, then thought over the possibilities. "Bill Groszkiewicz definitely won't miss him, I can tell you that. He lived next-door to Harry. They shared a property line and were always going at it about something." She lowered her voice. "There was also talk about a relationship between Bill and Sylvia—Harry's ex-wife—although I don't know how much of that's true and how much just neighborhood gossip. I do know, though, that Bill represented Sylvia when she left Harry last year." She chuckled again. "Whoo-ee! I bet Harry went through the roof when he found out Bill was Sylvia's lawyer!" She became serious again. "Don't get me wrong, though. Bill Groszkiewicz is a very fine man. I'd never suggest he'd physically harm anyone."

Sonny asked how Bill's last name was spelled and made a note of it.

"As long as you're talking to people," Mrs. Meyers went on, "I wouldn't leave out the poor fellow who's putting on Harry's roof. I'll bet *he* felt like killing Harry a couple of times. That young man's done a lot of work in this neighborhood and no one ever had problems with him before Harry." She ticked off names on her fingers. "He did Bill's roof in March, then he did the Patels', then the Smileys', then the Chens'. And now he's doing Harry's. It seems like that dirty old dump truck of his has been sitting on the street all spring. I realize it has to be there—it's for the debris from the old roof—but it's such an eyesore, and you can't help looking at it. It's been in front of Harry's house for five days now!"

Again she admonished, "But the roofer's a nice boy, and from what everybody except Harry says, his people do good work. I'm sure he didn't deserve the grief he was getting from Harry, but I'm not seriously suggesting he would have killed him."

φ

Sonny had intended his next stop to be a visit to Bill Groszkiewicz, but Mrs. Meyers informed him that Bill was on a Caribbean cruise for a week. So instead he paid a call on the roofer, Don Redfield. They arranged to meet at a job site.

Redfield was in his thirties, with an open, friendly face and light brown curls. "How about that explosion, huh?" he said after shaking hands with Sonny. "Looks like that's one roof we're not going to get paid for."

"That's a shame," said Sonny, "because I hear you spent a lot of time on that job. By the way, I thought a roof usually went on in a day or two. What took you so long this time?"

Spots of red appeared on the roofer's cheeks. "Cooper with his half-assed complaints, that's what." He lowered his voice and said tightly. "We've done a *lot* of jobs in that neighborhood and had *no* complaints. There was just no pleasing that guy Cooper. First he puts all these extra clauses in the contract, then comes out looking over my guys' shoulders every two minutes, making sure they 'do things right.' Like he knows how to put on a roof better than guys who have been doing it for twenty years! Then when we start replacing the plywood— which we had to do because some of the old stuff was rotten—he says he doesn't like the wood we're using. Wants us to get all new wood." The roofer rolled his eyes in disbelief. "That was a bunch of crap! The stuff we put in there was fine, it was better than code."

"Couldn't you just refuse to do it?"

"I wanted to, believe me. But Cooper kept saying he wasn't going to pay us if we didn't do things the way he wanted. And I didn't want to go to the trouble of taking him to court to make him pay." He added, "And to be honest, I didn't want to give him the excuse to go around bad-mouthing me to anybody who'd listen, because he was just the kind of guy who would do that. My company's small, but I'm starting to get a lot of work in this part of the county. I want to keep my good name." He shook his head. "I'll tell you, though, I'm sorry I ever took this job. I had a bad feeling about it when I was writing the contract. Think I'm gonna listen harder to my feelings next time."

φ

The next person Sonny tried to look up was the dead man's ex-wife, Sylvia. But it turned out she was in the Caribbean for a week, too. The neighborhood rumor mill might have gotten it right about Bill and Sylvia.

So instead, Sonny paid a call on Sylvia's sister, who lived nearby. The sister confirmed that Sylvia and Bill were indeed a couple now. She also supplied information about the divorce settlement. The court battle had been bitter, she said, but the settlement had been fair. Harry kept the house and Sylvia got their ocean-front condo. They split the businesses they owned: He took the pizza parlor and dry cleaner, she took the apartment building. They also split the stock portfolio. Fortunately for her, she'd sold her stocks before the market went belly-up, and now she was comfortably well-off.

φ

Back at the department Sonny shared his findings with his lieutenant. "I was disappointed to hear about the divorce settlement. My theory was that Sylvia got shafted and was holding a grudge, so she and her lawyer-boyfriend Bill hired somebody to get even with Harry while they were off on their cruise establishing an alibi. But the way it turned out, there's no obvious reason for revenge."

"How about the roofer? Was he mad enough at Cooper to blow up his house?"

"He sounded pretty mad, but he wouldn't get paid for the roofing job if the house disappeared— especially not if Harry disappeared with it. Although maybe Redfield figured he'd make out okay by charging off the unpaid bill on his taxes as a business loss. Also, if Harry's not around, he can't be bad-mouthing the roofing company."

"Seems like a little too much of a coincidence to me," commented the lieutenant. "The guy's house blows up at the same time he's having a fight with his roofer. Do some checking. See if this Redfield's got a record. Then get a list of his customers and see if you get any matches with the Suspicious Fires file. Maybe Redfield's gotten back at a bad customer before. The reports are all on the computer. You can just search on the names of the roofing-company customers."

Easy for you to say, thought Sonny as he grudgingly sat down in front of his computer again. But he found the Suspicious Fires file with surprisingly little trouble, then spent an easy ten minutes searching for hits on people who had gotten Roofs by Redfield. He had to admit the computer was an efficient way of searching the files—as long as people put enough detail into their reports. But in the end, no matches occurred between Redfield's customers and suspicious fires. And Redfield had never been arrested.

φ

With leads not panning out, Sonny decided to take another look at the video tape he'd gotten earlier from the TV station—film footage of the fire that followed the explosion, and of the people who had stood around watching it. This time he invited Harry Cooper's helpful neighbor to come down to the department and watch the video with him.

"Oh, there I am in my bathrobe," wailed Mrs. Meyers. "If I'd known I was going to be on TV I certainly would have gotten dressed first!" The truth was, she was barely noticeable among the other bystanders, most of whom were also in their nightclothes.

"What about this guy," asked Sonny, pointing to a person on the screen who was one of the exceptions. The tall, thin man had his hands in the pockets of a jeans jacket, and watched the scene with an inscrutable expression on his acne-scarred face. "Do you know him?"

Mrs. Meyers peered at the screen. "That looks like the fellow who delivers pizza. He must have been making a delivery and stayed around to watch the fire."

"Must have," agreed Sonny. But he thought: A pizza delivery at three o'clock in the morning?

φ

Sonny got the name of the pizza carry-out and paid a call. The manager apologized when he twice had to take phone calls during the interview. "Everybody's worried," he explained, "because we don't know what's going to happen to the business. You see, the owner was killed last week when his house blew up. You might have seen it on TV."

Interesting, thought Sonny as he recorded the coincidence in his notebook. He wrote himself a question: "Disgruntled employee?" Then he took out a still photo that had been made from the video tape, of the man in the jeans jacket watching the fire, and showed it to the manager.

"Yeah, he works for us," said the manager with a nod. "Name's Jacky Johnson. Not the friendliest guy in the world, but he's dependable, and he doesn't gripe about delivering to rough neighborhoods. If you want, I can give you his phone number and address."

Sonny took the information. But before he went in search of Jacky Johnson, he went back to the office and did another computer search. This time he got lots of hits. Johnson had been jailed for writing bad checks, breaking-and-entering, robbery, public drunkenness—and last but not least—arson. Lucky for the police—although unlucky for Jacky—he was apparently the kind of arsonist who liked to return to admire his handiwork.

In short order Sonny obtained a warrant and drove to Jacky's address, located in an uninspired grouping of garden apartments where the 'garden' was a neglected strip of mostly weeds. Sonny and the back-up officers he'd brought along climbed to the top floor. He knocked firmly on the metal door of 3C.

After a long moment, an unshaven Jacky opened the door. He gazed warily at the three policemen who confronted him, then stared with resignation at the warrant. Finally, he stood aside as they came in to search his unkempt one-bedroom apartment. In a closet, the searchers found a jeans jacket whose right sleeve was embedded with glass particles from the basement window of Harry's house, and in a kitchen drawer, a box of candles like the one used to set off the explosion. Sonny arrested Jacky for the murder of Harry Cooper.

φ

Two days later, Sonny was again working at his computer, this time with a look of satisfaction as he transferred the Cooper murder file to the Closed Cases directory. He was interrupted by a phone call from the public prosecutor's office, inviting him over for a visit.

"We thought you'd like to hear Jacky's statement," said the enthusiastic assistant prosecutor who greeted him when he arrived. She explained that Jacky originally claimed innocence, but finally decided to plea-bargain and tell them everything.

Jacky Johnson sat at a table in the prosecutor's office, looking downcast. "It was an accident," he said without raising his eyes.

"An accident you broke in and blew up the house?" asked Sonny with mock incredulity.

"No, I meant to do that. But no one was supposed to get hurt."

"Johnson says he was hired to destroy the house," broke in the assistant prosecutor, hoping to move the story along.

"Who hired him, the roofer?" asked Sonny. "Or was it the ex-wife and her boyfriend?"

"Wrong on both counts. It was Cooper himself."

Sonny stared at her blankly.

"Jacky," the senior prosecutor said with quiet authority, "why don't you just tell the story from the beginning."

Jacky sat up straight, now that he was the center of attention. "Harry knew about my police record when he hired me. He checked me out through my lease, because he owns the building I live in. He talked like he was doin' me a favor, said he liked to give ex-cons a second chance. But I figured out pretty soon he just liked havin' someone on his payroll that knew their way around and wasn't afraid of gettin' their hands dirty—for a couple extra bucks, that is. Like if Harry thought a supplier was cheatin' him, I'd go sabotage one of the guy's trucks. Or maybe set a little fire in a warehouse that would do a lot of smoke damage. Small stuff like that. I never killed anybody for him. I'm not a murderer.

"Anyway, couple weeks ago, Harry tells me he'll pay me a thousand bucks to torch a house, make it look like an accident. Drew me a picture of the layout, said he knew what it was like because the house was built just like his. When he said there was a gas stove, I knew how I was going to do the job—especially since he said the guy who lived there was gonna be out of town for a week. Because that meant nobody would get hurt if the place blew up."

"You mean he hired you to do *Groszkiewicz's* house?" said Sonny, unable to keep from interrupting.

"Yeah, Grosswit, whatever. Harry said he was pissed at the guy because here he's his next-door neighbor and he's helpin' his ex put the screws to him in court. But he said what *really* p.o.'ed him, was he was also the guy advised the ex to sell her share of the stocks, and she did it before the market tanked. Harry hung *on* to his!" Jacky gave either a grimace or a smile.

"Anyway," Jacky went on, "that was the name of the guy, Grosswit. Harry gave me the address. Turned out I already knew who the guy was. Delivered a pizza to him couple months ago. I remembered the godawful name—there couldn't be two of those—and I remembered the street real well because the houses all look the same and it's hard to see the numbers at night. So because of that, I figure I better make sure I know where I'm going, get the right house.

"Now what they make us do at the pizza shop, is the first time a customer orders, you ask for any special directions for finding the place, and you type it into the computer. That way, the next time they call in an order you don't have to waste time askin' for directions again. You just print out what's in the computer and slap it on the box. So before I go over there, I pull up this guy Growswit's name on the computer."

With an expression of contained excitement, the assistant prosecutor handed Sonny a computer-printed strip. "Apparently the first time Groszkiewicz ordered pizza was when he was getting a new roof put on."

Sonny took the strip and looked at it. Groszkiewicz's name and address were printed in blocky computer font, with the following tip: "Look for dump truck in front

φφφ

Verna Suit started life as an English major and went on to pick up arcane skills as an analyst with the Defense Department. In a second career as a freelance writer, she has written numerous magazine articles on the fiber arts and two non-fiction books: *Art Quilts: Playing with a Full Deck* (Pomegranate Artbooks, 1995) and *Potomac Craftsmen* (Crackle Press,

1996). Currently she reviews mystery novels for *Mystery Scene* magazine and *I Love a Mystery*, and coordinates a mystery review clipping service for Sisters in Crime. She also constructs crossword puzzles that appear in newspapers across the country, including *USA Today* and the *New York Times*.

VITAL SIGNS
by Marcia Talley

It was wrong. All wrong.

The helmet of bandages, the tubes and the wires, the machines that whirred and sighed and bleeped. I closed my eyes against the glare of the lights and the harsh reality of what lay beneath that thin, white blanket in intensive care. Lucy. *My* Aunt Lucy.

Behind my eyelids it was summertime. The honk of a car horn, the slap of a screen door and Aunt Lucy—all flowered aprons, broad smiles and damp, cinnamon-ginger hugs—waiting for me on the stoop. After Mother married Kyle the year I turned 10, she would park me at Aunt Lucy's farm the minute school let out in June. Kyle didn't take much to kids.

Those blissful summer days are gone now, and so are Mother and Kyle. When Uncle Chet died of

Parkinson's a few years back, he left just me, Aunt Lucy and Roy Allen, their son. Soon it would be just me and Roy. I didn't want to think about it.

The doctor laid a hand on my shoulder and guided me toward a chair. "Your aunt suffered massive head injuries, I'm afraid. The surgery helped alleviate the pressure on her brain, but..." He shrugged. "That tube in her windpipe is hooked up to a ventilator. It's breathing for her. We're monitoring her heart and her blood pressure, and she's being fed through that other tube you see in her nose. It's the best we can do." As he spoke, the ventilator cycled on and off, making a sound like air being released from a tire.

"I wish you had known her when..." *When she was alive*, I had started to say.

"She's the kindest woman I've ever known, doctor. Always taking in strays." I swallowed hard, wondering if one of Aunt Lucy's strays had turned on her. "Back home, when Harry Emerson lost his job at the bank? She invited him to move into the old tenant house with his three disabled sons. Harry'd do odd jobs for her, but she refused to let him pay rent. Then there was this deaf kid, Sheila Sue. When she was 16, my aunt hired her as a part-time housekeeper; even paid to send her to a special school in Washington, D.C. And Peg!" I smiled at the memory of my aunt's semi-reluctant, one-legged farmhand. "She even rescued the town hobo..."

I rattled on and on.

The doctor probably thought it'd be therapeutic because he nodded sympathetically, patted my hand once or twice and otherwise showed no signs of being in a hurry to leave.

"She'll make it." I was reassuring myself as much as him. "She's a tough lady. She used to say that if she could make it through the Depression, she could make it through anything."

"Are you her next of kin?" he asked.

"That'd be her son, my cousin, Roy." I gathered up my sweater and my handbag and we walked out the door together. "I've already called him. He's flying in from Tennessee tomorrow."

Roy came, but he didn't stay for long. "There's nothing I can do here, B.R.," he told me after only one day. "Besides, I gotta get back to work." He made it sound so reasonable. He had important clients to take care of, surely I could understand that, and some hot real estate deal on the front burner. If that fell through, he explained, there wouldn't be any money to pay the hospital bills.

"You check in with Mother and let me know if there's any change. Call me right away. You will, won't you?" He was standing half in the hall, holding the door open with one hand. His brown suit was rumpled, as if he had slept in it, and the blue eyes behind his glasses were rimmed with red. "If there's anything she needs..."

"Sure, Roy, sure," I said. But I was thinking very un-Christian thoughts. "You S.O.B.!" I wanted to shout. "Running out on her again. Always expecting me to pick up the pieces. As if I didn't have a life. And a parish to take care of."

My cousin stepped back into the room and gave me a one-armed hug, his chin resting for a moment on the top of my head. "Thanks, B.R." I had just opened my mouth to remind him that my name is Bailey Rose, if you please, but he had already gone.

I came to visit Aunt Lucy every day after that, although they wouldn't let me stay for long. I'd sit by her bed and reminisce, retelling family stories that used to make us laugh. Often as I talked I'd pick up one of her hands where it lay limply on the blanket, hold it and stroke it, the flesh thin and smooth and loose, moving easily, too easily over her bones. Skin so delicate that I thought it might tear. Stroking gently and wondering *who would do such a thing?*

It had happened so fast. A neighbor at Holiday Hills had dialed 911 within seconds of finding my aunt and as soon as the ambulance screamed out of the parking lot, had telephoned me at St. Stephen's where I was putting the finishing touches on my sermon for Sunday. The police were still there, the woman reported, complaining about the way the paramedics had messed up the crime scene while trying to save my aunt's life.

At the hospital, a detective came to see me because I'm listed on the form at the retirement home. He was hoping she'd come out of the coma. He wanted to get a statement. "Detective Martinez." He extended a hand. "Fa...? Reverend? Ma'am?"

There was an uncomfortable silence while he took in my black suit, gray shirt and white dog collar. It's a reaction I'm used to by now. "Ms. Lawrence will do just fine." I smiled.

"Sorry about your mother," he said, tucking his hat under his arm.

"She's my aunt."

"Oh." He shifted his weight from one leg to the other, as if his feet hurt. "Well, ma'am, we think your aunt interrupted a burglary in progress. Looks like she'd just come in with the groceries. We found a torn paper bag. Food scattered all over the floor. And her pocketbook was missing. Place was a mess. They really tossed it." He glanced over his shoulder at Aunt Lucy and shook his head. "Bastards didn't have to kill her."

"She's not dead yet," I reminded him.

He had the decency, at least, to look embarrassed. When he spoke again, his voice was softer, with the edge knocked off. "We've dusted for prints, Ms. Lawrence, but we really don't expect to find anything. Whoever did it probably wore gloves." He handed me his card. "Please call me if she comes to." He paused. "Or if anything changes."

He expected her to die. They all did, even the paramedics who were first on the scene. Shortly after surgery, when the nurse first hooked Aunt Lucy up to the IVs and the monitors, one of the EMTs stopped by. He stood just inside the door for a few moments, heavy work gloves clutched in one hand. When he turned to go, he noticed me for the first time. "Oh, sorry! I just wanted to see how she's doing." He looked toward the bed. "You know, we thought she was dead. Her head was all…" He touched his temple. "Well, there was an awful lot of blood and she wasn't breathing. My partner said, 'She's gone, man' but me, what do I know? First week on the job. It coulda been my grandma lying there! I had to do something!" He confessed that he had never performed CPR on a real patient before, just practice on a dummy. Though nearly exhausted, he and his partner had kept it up all the way to the hospital.

He smiled. "I guess I saved her life, huh?"

"Yes, you did," I said. "And I'm very grateful."

He glanced sideways at my aunt, taking in the motionless cocoon of bandages. "I'm wondering now if it was worth it."

"I don't know," I told him truthfully.

I was feeling responsible, too. If it hadn't been for me, she wouldn't have been here at all. Aunt Lucy had been thinking about leaving the farm, moving to one of those life-care communities. She came here because of the weather. Thought she'd give Tampa a try. "But I don't like it," she'd told me after her third month. "It's so relentlessly...pleasant. I miss the mountains and the smell of new-mown hay and the way the mist lies on the fields in the morning. God help me, I even miss the damn frogs. When the lease is up, Rosie, I'm going home."

Seven days after they brought her in, I thought her wish might come true—Aunt Lucy opened her eyes. The doctor called me at church with the good news. "She's out of the coma, Ms. Lawrence." But then he socked me with the bad. "But, she's suffering from aphasia, I'm afraid. She can't talk. She may sometimes appear to be awake and alert, she may even look at you, but she doesn't seem to be able to transform her thoughts into speech."

I hurried to the hospital to see for myself. As I passed the nurse's station on my way to Aunt Lucy's room, I asked for details. "How's she doing?"

"I think you'll be pleased." Nurse Jacobs looked up from a chart, while her pen still scribbled away. "All those prayers must be working. Several times this morning I caught her following me with her eyes, and I've noticed that she's shifted around a bit in the bed. But she seems to be having spasms in her hands and feet. Not surprising, though, considering the extent of her injuries." She slipped the pen into the pocket of her uniform and smiled at me sympathetically. "I keep thinking how hard it must be for you, Ms. Lawrence, coming here day after day, seeing your aunt in this condition. All those hours you've spent with her! If you don't mind my asking, what do you find to talk about?"

"I apologize, mostly. For being such a pig-headed kid." I smiled, remembering. There was always plenty of work to do on the farm but I was usually off in a world of my own, climbing trees or chasing fireflies, or with my nose stuck in a book. I never managed to clean my room or do my assigned chores on time. But even if she had to remind me over and over, Aunt Lucy never lost her patience.

I was expecting a miracle, of course, so I was disappointed when I saw her—Aunt Lucy appeared to be sleeping. I stooped to kiss her forehead and to tuck away a wisp of silver hair that had escaped from the bandage. When her eyes suddenly opened, I was so startled that my heart thudded hard against my ribs and my stomach lurched and I wanted to shout, Hooray! but I grabbed the cold metal frame of the bed instead, squeezed tight and said, as calmly as I could, "Hi, Aunt Lucy. Welcome back." I caressed her cheek. "I knew you were in there somewhere, just waiting to get out."

"Do you mind?" Detective Martinez materialized out of nowhere, almost as if he had been lurking behind the door, scaring the bejezzus out of me. "The doc said this might work." Against my objections, he held a smooth, white tablet up in front of my aunt. "Who did this to you?"

Aunt Lucy kept dropping the Magic Marker he gave her to write with so Nurse Jacobs brought in a board with the alphabet painted on it. With an unsteady finger, Aunt Lucy pointed out "Q,P,M,X" before I made Martinez stop. "Go away," I pleaded. "Can't you see she's not up to this?" and I had to go around to the other side of the privacy curtain so Aunt Lucy wouldn't see me cry.

After Martinez packed up and left, promising to return the next day, I dragged the only chair in the room over to the bed, fell back into it and started talking. About anything. About nothing. About how wonderful it would be when she got better. About books we'd read, shows we'd see, trips we'd take with Roy and his wife.

Suddenly, tears began to gather in Aunt Lucy's eyes, filling them, spilling over, rolling sideways down her cheeks and onto the pillow. Her right hand, the one not connected to the IV, began to move spasmodically as if picking lint off the blanket.

"It's OK," I told her, trying my best to sound convincing. "You're going to be fine."

Aunt Lucy struggled to raise her hand from the blanket, her frail body trembling with the effort. She crossed her fingers as if making a wish. Then she made a tight fist. Crossed her fingers again. Made a fist. Her eyes remained locked on mine. She did not blink.

"Sweet Jesus God," I whispered. "Sweet God almighty!" I grabbed her hand and pressed it to my lips. "I'll be back in a minute, Auntie."

In seconds, I was out the door. I interrupted the nurse who was talking on the telephone. "Nurse!" I shouted, "Nurse Jacobs! I fumbled for the business card that was still in the pocket of my sweater. "Here!" I plopped the card down on the counter in front of her and jabbed at it with my finger. "Call that police officer right away. Tell him to get over here, and tell him to bring someone who understands sign language. Those weren't muscle spasms you saw. My aunt is finger spelling and she wants to tell us something!"

φ

"She must have learned sign language from Sheila Sue, her deaf housekeeper," I told Detective Martinez before the interpreter arrived. "I know a few letters, is all. It's R-A, officer. Over and over. She's asking for R.A."

"What's R.A?" he asked.

"It's a who," I told him. "Her son, Roy Allen. We called him R.A. as a kid. She's making other signs now, but I don't know what they are."

Neither of us was aware that the interpreter had entered the room behind us until she spoke. "She's saying, 'R.A. was angry. He hit me again and again. I begged him…'"

Unexpectedly, Aunt Lucy's hands fell to her sides, the fingers relaxed and I saw that her eyes had closed. I rushed to the bed and rattled the safety rail. "No!" I shouted. "Aunt Lucy! Don't die!"

Nurse Jacobs glanced at the monitors and touched my arm. "Don't worry. She's just fallen asleep. The effort's exhausted her, poor thing."

That evening, they arrested Roy Allen at his home in Nashville. He would be extradited to Florida and charged with the attempted murder of his mother, Lucille Norton Lawrence. Roy Allen hadn't been very bright. He had argued over the fare with the cabby who'd driven him from the airport to his mother's apartment. The cabby remembered him particularly because he didn't carry any luggage, not even a briefcase, and he hadn't left a tip. When confronted with an American Airlines passenger list with his name printed on it plain as day, Roy confessed. He couldn't have his mother moving back to the farm, he told Detective Martinez, because there wasn't any farm to move back to. When his father was first diagnosed with Parkinson's disease, Roy had persuaded his parents to put the farm into a trust in order to protect his mother's assets. They made Roy sole trustee. Then Roy had some half-baked scheme to build a shopping center and he'd put up the farm as collateral; when the shopping center failed and he couldn't make the payments, the bank had foreclosed.

Roy goes to trial sometime next month and he says he'll plead guilty, but that doesn't make it any easier on his wife and the kids, or on me.

As for my aunt, she seemed drained after that, as if every ounce of strength, every reserve had been expended in the effort to wake up and tell us what happened. She relapsed. She faded away, like the stars in a dawn sky.

Yesterday, I visited Aunt Lucy for the last time. I was reading to her from the Sunday section of the *Tampa Tribune* when those fragile, expressive hands which hadn't stirred for days suddenly began to move. One hand, palm down, made repeated circles—*Please, please*—on her chest. With the fingers of her right hand she formed a crooked "V" and plucked at her left, then, with obvious effort, laced the fingers of both hands together and wiggled them up and down.

The interpreter, summoned from the hospital cafeteria where she had been having lunch, watched for a few minutes, waiting patiently while my aunt shakily unlaced her fingers and extended her hands, turning the right palm up and the left palm down. The interpreter leaned forward and her own hands began to move, in a slow, fluid ballet. "I'm telling your aunt that I understand."

"Yes, yes," I pressed. "But what's she *saying?*"

Aunt Lucy turned toward me with wet and pleading eyes as the interpreter translated, "'I love you, Rosie. Now, please, unplug the machine and let me die.'"

Many tearful prayers later, for once in my life, I did exactly what Aunt Lucy wanted me to do the very first time she asked

φφφ

Marcia Talley is the award-winning author of *Through The Darkness* (Morrow/Avon, 2006) and five previous Hannah Ives mysteries, all set in Maryland. She is author/editor of two star-studded collaborative serial novels from St. Martins Press, *Naked Came The Phoenix* and *I'd Kill For That,* set in a fashionable health spa and an exclusive gated community, respectively. Her short stories appear in more than a dozen collections including "Too Many Cooks," a humorous retelling of Shakespeare's Macbeth from the viewpoint of the three witches which won both the Agatha and Anthony awards. A recent story, "Driven to Distraction" from Chesapeake Crimes II also won an Agatha and is featured in *The Deadly Bride and 21 of the Year's Finest Crime and Mystery Stories* (Carroll and Graf, 2006).

Marcia lives in Annapolis, Maryland, with a husband who loves to sail and a cat who doesn't.

WEDDING KNIFE
by Elaine Viets

The bride stood at the altar, a vision of white lace and billowing silk skirts. Suddenly, she collapsed at Father McLauren's feet, the white silk skirts spreading across the floor like spilled cream.

"Gail!" I said, rushing over to her, but the priest and the groom were already there, trying to revive her.

"Stand back," said Father McLauren, with the authority of a man who had had twenty years' experience with skittish brides. "Give her some air."

The wedding party, five bridesmaids and five groomsmen, all stepped back. As maid of honor, I hovered a fraction closer than the others. It was my duty to attend to the bride.

Slowly, Gail revived, her face as white as her wedding dress, and not nearly as pretty. She sat up. "Where am I?" she said, in a dazed voice.

"You're at St. Philomena's, getting married," Father McLauren said, smiling gently.

"Shit!" said the bride, loud enough so the first pews heard her. I could hear her mother gasp. It was Gail's mother who had pushed for this wedding to Harold Humphrey IV. It was Gail's mother who was hot for Handsome Harry's social connections, not to mention his money. Gail went along with it because she was twenty-nine, it was "time to get married," and if she had to get married it was better to marry a rich man than a poor one.

And Gail had to get married. She was four months' gone, and way too Catholic to even consider abortion. That was probably why she'd fainted. She was pregnant, too sick to eat anything but soda crackers and 7-Up, and Gail's mother had laced her into the dress so tightly she could hardly breathe. But Gail's mother didn't want any ugly rumors. She would try to pass off the baby as "premature," not that anyone but her would care.

The groom went along with the wedding plans because he was thirty-five and it was time he started producing the fifth Harold Humphrey. He was getting family pressure, the kind that resulted in his allowance being cut off. But nobody, except maybe his bride, expected Handsome Harry to be faithful. The man had a roving eye and a wicked little curl that hung down on his forehead. Men who looked like that were meant to stray.

The priest gave the bride a sharp look, and I wondered if he was going to tell her it wasn't too late to call off the wedding. But Gail spoke up quickly. "I'm sorry, Father," she said. "I shouldn't have said that in church. I was embarrassed because I'd made a fool of myself by fainting. I should have eaten breakfast. I apologize for my language. I'm ready to get married now."

It was the priest who helped Gail up, not the groom. I came forward and straightened Gail's dress and ten-foot seed pearl train. Her Alencon lace veil slid to one side, so I righted that, too. Through the white lace over her face, I thought I caught the faint tracks of tears, sliding down her hundred-dollar makeup job.

I would have felt pity for her, but I couldn't forgive her for what she'd done to me. Gail had made me a laughing stock in this despicable dress. The other bridesmaids were little blonde Barbie dolls. I was tall and dramatically brunette. Put me in a dark dress with long, clean lines and I looked sleek and sophisticated. But this getup was pink—pink, like a frigging prom dress. It had ruffles all over, and to make it worse, it had a tiny white lace jacket that ended under the armpits. The little blonde bridesmaids looked dainty in pink ruffles. I looked like a linebacker in lace. I begged Gail to let me wear a more becoming style—maids of honor often did wear a different dress from the bridesmaids. But two of Harry's sisters, Junie and Jill, were in the wedding, and they loved the pink ruffled dress. Gail's younger sisters, Heather and Ashley agreed. The four blonde twits insisted that we all had to wear the same thing to "look right."

Nothing would ever make me look right in that outfit.

"Come on, Vanessa," Gail said, trying to soothe me in the dress shop. "We went to high school together. You know all bridesmaids' dresses are hopeless. You can make me wear something horrible when you get married." She thought it was funny.

"That will never happen," I said. "I'm not the marrying kind."

I wasn't, either. I preferred married men. No muss, no fuss, no proposals to spoil the fun. I enjoyed sneaking around, and when I got bored with the affair, I broke it off. The men didn't dare complain, or try to get me back. They didn't want their wives finding out.

So although I felt sorry for Gail, I took a small secret delight in her discomfort. What are friends for?

The rest of the wedding went off without a hitch. Harry pulled back his bride's lace veil and kissed her with a show of passion that left the old women in the front pews fanning themselves. I handed Gail her heavy bouquet of white roses and the oddly appropriate baby's breath, and straightened her seed pearl train again when she turned to face the congregation. Everyone applauded the new Mr. and Mrs. Humphrey.

Then came countless photos and the videotaping, while the wedding guests loitered outside the church. I hated posing for pictures, and wondered if I could offer the photographer something to ruin the pictures of me in that dress. I'd caught a glimpse of myself in a mirror in the brides' room at the church, and saw it was worse than I thought.

At last we ran down the church steps while the guests blew politically correct bubbles (rice hurt the little birdies) and into the waiting white limos.

The reception was lavish. It was held in the main ballroom of the old Mauldin hotel, a fantasy of white and gold trimmed with ten thousand dollars' worth of flowers. My Aunt Marlene had finagled an invitation. Of course, she couldn't resist a jab at me in the receiving line. "That's the ugliest bridesmaid's dress I've ever seen," she said, "and I've seen some in my time."

Aunt Marlene was about eighty. Her skin was spotted with warts, moles, and age spots until she looked like a fat speckled hen, with a yellow beak of a nose. The wrinkles under her chin folded up and down like an accordion when she talked. She was wearing her all-purpose navy blue wedding and funeral dress with the rhinestone buttons.

"Thanks, Aunt Marlene. You always know how to make a girl feel good," I said.

"I always tell the truth," she said, righteously. "I know my duty."

"And never shirked it, either," I said.

"That's right," she said, ignoring the dig. "And what was that Gail doing cursing on the altar? Disrespectful, I call it."

Exciting, I'd call it. I hadn't seen such malice light up those old dead lizard eyes since Mrs. Dougherty ran off with the Scoutmaster.

"She fainted," I said.

"I'll bet she's pregnant," said Aunt Marlene, and I knew that no matter how tight Gail was laced, Aunt Marlene wouldn't be fooled when the baby came along.

Finally, the receiving line was over. The wedding party scattered to grab a drink, put their bouquets down or use the bathroom. Gail look beat. "I need to sit down for a minute," she said.

"Are you OK?" I asked her.

"Yeah, sure," she said, managing a weak smile. "Just some last minute jitters up there at the altar."

"Can I get you anything? Water? Some food?" The groom should have done this, but he was nowhere to be seen.

"Shoes," she said. "These satin heels are killing me. We still have to throw the bouquet and the garter, cut the cake and dance. Would you get me my comfortable shoes? I stashed them in the back storage room, by the band stand."

She pointed in that direction, and I trotted over and opened the door. The light was already on. I saw stacks of beer kegs and soda cases, and a shelf with things the bride would need that night—some lipstick and tissues, a brush and hair spray, comfortable shoes, a short dress she could change into later, and the ornamental cake knife. The storage room angled off to the right.

And there, against a back counter, was the groom, getting his own private reception from Ashley, and it was a warm one. In fact, they were consummating their new position as in-laws. They didn't notice me. I grabbed Gail's shoes off the shelf, tiptoed out, shut the door —and ran straight into Aunt Marlene.

"What got into you? You're white as a sheet," she said.

"Nothing," I said, shakily.

"You're lying," Aunt Marlene said, and her chins wobbled like Jell-O in an earthquake. Her old eyes narrowed, and the net of wrinkles around them gathered tighter. "He's in there with his own sister-in-law, isn't he?"

"How did you know?" I said. Aunt Marlene didn't miss much.

"I saw him sneak in there, and five minutes later, I saw her, looking just as sneaky. I knew they were up to no good. I think Gail saw him, too, and that's why she sent you in there for her shoes."

"I better get these to her," I said, hoping I could get away, but Aunt Marlene clamped her hand on my arm.

"I hope this marriage lasts until I've paid off their present on my Penney's charge," she said, ominously.

With that, the photographer, who called the shots at all weddings these days, announced it was time to throw the bouquet. Gail had a special "throwing bouquet" made up so she could have the white roses dried and preserved. I handed it to her, then slipped away. I'd made her promise that she wouldn't throw the bouquet to me or make a spectacle out of me. I liked my single status.

When I came back, the girlish squealing had stopped and Harry's sister Jill had caught the bouquet, amid general cheers. "They were fighting over it," said Aunt Marlene. "A regular scrimmage."

"Where's the groom?" said the photographer. "It's time to throw the garter."

"Yes, where is the groom?" said Jill and Heather. Ashley said nothing. She looked flushed and her hair was coming out of its French twist, and I didn't think it was from the battle over the bouquet.

Gail glared at her guilty sister. The tension was so thick, you could cut it with a knife.

"I'll get him," said Gail grimly, and it sounded like a threat. She marched straight across to the storage room, flung open the door, and slammed it behind her.

Soon after that, we heard her screams. The bride came out drenched in bright blood, her silk and Alencon lace dress splashed with red. There were sprays of red across her face and veil, and her eyes were wide with shock. She was holding a long, heavy silver knife in her hand. Blood dripped down it and onto her sleeves. She looked like a creature in a horror movie.

"The wedding cake knife!" someone screamed, and then I saw the blood-drenched bouquet of ribbons and lily of the valley at the handle.

"Gracious, that girl stabbed her own husband," said Aunt Marlene, nearly delirious with delighted malice. She'd never had such a show for the price of a Penney's jelly dish with a silver-plate spoon. "Not that he didn't deserve it, philandering at his own reception."

"No!" I said. "No, it's not true. She didn't do it."

But now I heard the screams of the groom's mother. Her handsome Harry boy was dead, blood all over his starched white pleated shirt and black tuxedo. She couldn't explain why his cummerbund was in his hand. She thought it must have come loose and he'd retired to the storage room to fix it. I couldn't bring myself to go into the storage room again, but Aunt Marlene did, and she gave me all the details. She also spread the word that Harry had been in there alone with his own sister-in-law, doing unspeakable things. Which Aunt Marlene was more than happy to speak about.

The friends of the bride and the groom divided themselves into two camps, as if someone had drawn a line down the middle of the ballroom. There were tears and angry voices on each side. Naturally, Harry's family blamed the bride, but I maintained she was innocent. She did nothing but cry. Her father, who was a lawyer, told her not to say a word when the police got there.

We stayed at the reception until after midnight, but there was no dancing or dinner. We were all forced to stay there and talk to the police. I didn't tell them what I'd seen in the storage room, but that didn't do Gail any good. Aunt Marlene blabbed to the cops, and the police came back to me and threatened me with obstruction of justice unless I talked. The groom had been carried out in a black body bag hours ago, and I was still there. The weeping bride was handcuffed and carted off to jail, but the cops kept her bloody dress as evidence.

Her father had enough clout to get her out on bail and enough money to get her the best defense attorney.

The details of the autopsy were so disgraceful, Aunt Marlene had to whisper them when she told all the neighbors—and me.

"The autopsy showed the groom had had sex just before his death, and not with the bride. At least, those weren't her blonde hairs they found on him," Aunt Marlene said, shivering with glee.

"Anyone could have left blonde hair on him. He was kissed by a lot of women in the receiving line," I said.

"No, they were female hairs from 'down there,'" Aunt Marlene said, each whisper a stab in

Gail's back. "And they found stains and things. He'd been with another woman at his wedding reception. No wonder Gail stabbed him. There won't be a woman in this town who blames her."

"I don't care what they found," I said. "She didn't do it."

"You're loyal to a fault," Aunt Marlene said.

φ

By the time of the trial, Gail was eight-and-a-half months pregnant. Her attorney shrewdly insisted the trial go on. Tests had proved the baby was the groom's, and she had the sympathy of every woman on the jury—and most of the men, too. The defense had done its homework, and made sure there were several fathers with daughters. They wanted to kill Harry all over again.

I had to testify to what I saw, thanks to Aunt Marlene's big mouth.

The bride swore she was innocent.

I think if Gail had told the jury she stabbed Harry in a fit of rage, they would have understood and set her free. But she said she didn't do it, that she walked in there and saw the knife in his chest and heard him trying to breathe. She pulled the knife out and that's how she got blood all over herself.

The jury didn't like that. They didn't mind that she killed Harry, but they hated that she lied about it. Still, they couldn't be too mad at the poor girl. They only convicted her of manslaughter, and she got the minimum sentence. Her mother will watch the baby when it is born, although her in-laws have sued for custody. I don't think they'll get it, but I do think the kid will get the Humphrey millions in trust.

And Gail was innocent, even if no one believed her.

Because if Harry got lucky at the reception, well, so did I. No one saw me go in the storage room the second time. They were too busy watching who caught the bouquet. I went in there to tell Harry exactly what I thought of him.

I was already unhappy when I caught him in there with that simp Ashley. I didn't mind sharing him with his wife—as I said, I liked married men. But I hated that he had another lover, when he'd promised I would be the only one. Of course I should have known. Harry had just promised to love, honor and obey Gail, and he'd broken those vows in an hour.

Anyway, I went back in that storage room and told him what I thought of him. And Harry said, "Can you blame me for cheating on you, Vanessa? You look like a drag queen in that dress."

So I picked up the wedding cake knife and stabbed him in the chest. I didn't mean to do it, but once it happened, I couldn't undo it. Fortunately, there was very little blood. The knife held it in. I thought he was dead, but I was wrong. Harry was just barely alive when his bride came in. She pulled the knife out, trying to save him. Of course that was what killed him. Everyone but Gail knew you're supposed to leave the knife in when someone's stabbed like that. When she pulled it out, Harry's blood sprayed all over his bride. When Gail walked out of the storage room drenched in red, it looked like she'd killed him.

None of it would have happened if she'd let me wear a different bridesmaid's dress.

Gail served only two years of a four-year sentence. I consider that just. I think any woman who's ever had to wear an ugly bridesmaid's dress would agree.

φφφ

Elaine Viets writes two bestselling mystery series. *Murder Unleashed* is her newest Dead End Job novel for NAL. She also writes the Josie Marcus Mystery Shopper series. *High Heels Are Murder* is the latest Josie book.

Elaine is the author of numerous short stories. "Wedding Knife" won both the Anthony and the Agatha Awards. She must confess that her own bridesmaids wore orange chiffon harem pants. (Hey, it was the 1970s.)

CPSIA information can be obtained
at www.ICGtesting.com
Printed in the USA
LVHW041709260819
628958LV00003B/331

9 781430 305255